"Where do you think you're taking me?"

Denise tilted the rearview mirror to reflect her face back at him. Vulnerability flicked in her topaz eyes. Then her lids lowered, and he questioned whether the vulnerability had been there at all. He must have been mistaken.

"I thought you might help me track your wife's killer."

The reminder that a murderer was still at large burned Ford's stomach like acid. "Help you how?"

"I'm used to tracking cheating husbands and divorcés who avoid meeting their financial obligations to their ex-wives and children, not going after killers. And I don't have your business or social connections."

A lot of good his money and networking had done him when he'd tried to find the assassin. "I hired the best private investigators. None of them turned up a clue."

Pride and a hint of challenge entered Denise's tone. "You should have hired me."

Dear Reader,

You're about to return to the Braddacks' world of privilege, wealth and intrigue. In this, the spin-off of Susan Kearney's *Lullaby Deception*, you'll meet up with the second Braddack twin, Ford.

Imagine a groom kidnapped by a spunky private investigator, imagine an assassin, and a chase in which one misplaced step could bring death. Add sizzling sexual attraction and you have the kind of suspenseful read you expect from Susan Kearney.

Susan lives in a Tampa suburb with her husband of sixteen years, her two children and two Boston terriers. She graduated with a business degree from the University of Michigan, where she was a three-time all-American diver. Susan is currently at work on her next Intrigue novel.

Now join Ford Braddack as he searches for his wife's killer...and finds a new love.

Happy reading!

Sincerely,

Debra Matteucci
Senior Editor & Editorial Coordinator
Harlequin Books
300 East 42nd Street
New York, New York 10017

Sweet Deception
Susan Kearney

Harlequin Books

**TORONTO • NEW YORK • LONDON
AMSTERDAM • PARIS • SYDNEY • HAMBURG
STOCKHOLM • ATHENS • TOKYO • MILAN
MADRID • WARSAW • BUDAPEST • AUCKLAND**

For Denise O'Sullivan, my editor, with many thanks
for her support and encouragement, for her honest
enthusiasm to make my work the best possible,
and most of all for her faith in me.

ISBN 0-373-22428-1

SWEET DECEPTION

Copyright © 1997 by Susan Kearney

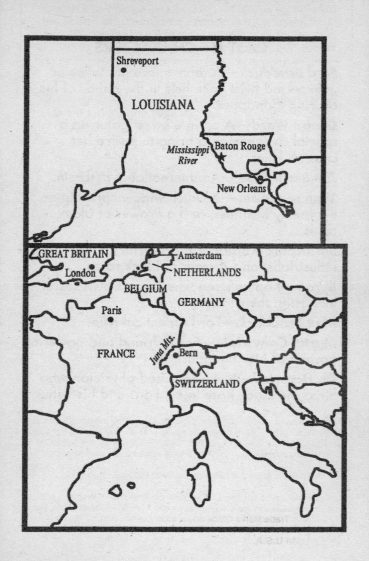

CAST OF CHARACTERS

Ford Braddack—A man whose life takes an unexpected twist once he's in the hands of his alluring kidnapper.

Denise Ward—A private investigator on a special assignment to bring to justice her cousin's killer.

The Black Rose—An international assassin.

Yvonne Jansen—A Dutch widow carrying on the family business, and a grower of black roses.

Sir Richard Kaplan—A powerful English industrialist and grower of black roses.

Byron—Kaplan's son who has his own secret interest in the rare black roses.

Max Braddack—Ford's identical twin.

Martin Crewsdale—Ford's friend and powerful partner at Norton Industries.

Dr. Henschel—Now-deceased physician who hired the Black Rose to kill Ford and his wife.

Prologue

All she had left to do was kidnap the groom. Denise Ward had finished the distasteful chore of paying the bride to leave town. She'd called the guests to inform them of the wedding's cancellation and had made a donation to the minister's favorite charity.

Consulting the notes on her desk, she reread the September schedule she'd committed to memory. Since Ford Braddack's private jet wasn't due in New Orleans from Beijing until tomorrow morning, the groom shouldn't learn of the changes she'd made in his wedding plans until it was too late.

Denise shifted in her lumpy chair, hoping Ford didn't kill her once he discovered what she'd done. Ford Braddack was unpredictable, had the devil's own temper. According to her investigations, his wife's death last year had made him even more abrupt, demanding and domineering than usual, so she had no way to predict how he'd respond to his canceled wedding or his kidnapping.

Not only did he work impossibly long hours, the man drove his employees hard, and he played hard, too. Ford had grieved deeply after Rhonda's death, disappearing for a while, then throwing himself into the company with a ruthlessness that shot Norton Industries' stock soaring. His corporate exploits hadn't slowed during the past six months. Although he'd escorted a variety of debutantes to business functions, charity events and to his home in the exclusive Garden District, no woman ever stayed the night in his mansion.

Denise closed the file on her desk and stared unseeing out the window. One month ago, Lindsay Betancourt had whirled into Ford's life with the force of a hurricane. Two weeks ago, Ford had announced his engagement. Denise had been hired to contain the destruction.

She imagined him furiously conducting business now, fully expecting to marry Lindsay tomorrow.

But Denise had canceled the wedding.

Abductions weren't her regular line of work. Her usual cases involved following cheating husbands and chasing down hiding divorcés behind on child support and alimony—a far less dangerous task. While her P.I. firm might be in desperate need of the cash this assignment provided, Denise had accepted the contract only after discovering that Miss Lindsay Betancourt didn't care one whit for Ford Braddack. While the scheming woman had claimed a deep affection for Ford, she'd jumped at the substantial bribe Denise's client had offered her to leave New Orleans for Hollywood.

Only God knew how Ford would react once he discovered the betrayal—not only Denise's, but her client's. Apprehension, mixed with the thrill of anticipation, clutched at her stomach. Her neck itched,

warning her to watch her step and keep her distance.
When Ford's business ran smoothly, he was a man to
be reckoned with. She shuddered to think how he'd
react to her kidnapping him from his own wedding.

Chapter One

A groom should be happy or at least eager on his wedding day, but roiling thunderclouds reflected Ford's mood. Thirty weeks and four days had passed since his wife had died in the avalanche. He ought to be able to accept her death. But he couldn't.

Adjusting his bow tie, he looked in the mirror and scowled at the dark circles under his eyes. What had happened to his renowned control? Since he'd awakened from a coma to learn of his beloved wife's murder, he'd functioned by ruthlessly suppressing his grief. As he slipped into the black jacket of his tuxedo and tugged on the cuffs, he couldn't help remembering how Rhonda's eyes had shone with pleasure as she'd performed the wifely task for him.

His inability to sleep most nights would disappear with his new marriage. Lindsay Betancourt would make a fine wife, easing the sadness and loneliness that weighed on his heart. He had to accept he would never love another woman like his Rhonda and shed the sorrow that weighed like lead on his chest. He had to move on, recover, get on with his life.

He didn't regret giving Lindsay carte blanche over

the wedding arrangements when it had made her so happy. If she'd asked his opinion, he'd have chosen a quiet ceremony with only family and close friends, instead of the extravaganza she'd planned. And he'd much prefer driving his sports car rather than riding in his company's stretch limo. But she'd planned the frilly details and hadn't asked anything of him but to show up at the church on time.

He straightened his collar with distaste. Yet if wearing this tight-necked monkey suit made Lindsay happy, he'd do it, grateful for such an easy way to indulge her. Determined to make a success of this marriage, he shoved aside his brooding over last-minute doubts. All grooms had second thoughts. With strict, practiced control of his emotions, he thrust his reservations aside. He'd spoil Lindsay, and in return, perhaps his loneliness would ease.

Checking his watch, Ford frowned. Where was the limousine?

Patting his pocket to ensure he had the rings to give to Max, his identical twin and best man, Ford rolled his luggage outside because the staff had the week off. The security system was activated. He'd cleared his desk of work for the week. Determined not to show up late for his wedding, he waited, impatient for the limo to arrive.

Gray thunderheads furrowed the Louisiana sky. Steamy humidity clung to his flesh and dampened his clothes. Lightning zigzagged earthward and thunderclaps warned of an early fall storm. As Ford walked from the shelter of the house, the skies opened, spattering the brick walkway with fat droplets.

Finally. The white limousine pulled through the

electronically opened wrought-iron gates and onto his driveway. He didn't recognize the uniformed chauffeur from the company driving pool who without a word of greeting, exited the vehicle, his face hidden by a cap drawn low over his face. The driver produced an umbrella and held open the passenger door while Ford slipped into the car.

He'd barely seated himself and brushed the stray drops of rain from his hair before the door slammed with an ominous thud. The driver carelessly tossed the luggage into the trunk. Ford opened his mouth to complain, but hail the size of marbles pelted the car's roof, setting off an enormous din. He fastened his seat belt, and as the driver jerked away from the curb, Ford glanced at the car door.

The handle was gone.

His gaze darted to the far door. Another missing handle. The hardware's absence was no coincidence. The prickling hairs on his neck turned to a full-fledged stab of alarm. He couldn't open the door from inside the vehicle.

Despite the hail pinging against the roof, he pressed the electric window switch. The glass didn't budge. What the hell was going on?

Looking out the window at the familiar route to the church, his temper welled up like lava. While the New Orleans downpour might be normal, this limo ride was not. He lifted the phone, and found the instrument dead. And as for trying to break out a window, he knew the car came equipped with bulletproof glass. Until someone from outside opened the car door, he was incarcerated. He commanded thousands of employees with a crook of his finger, transferred millions of dollars with a punch of a button, but he couldn't control where his damn car took him.

He rerouted his rippling anger into precise constructive analysis, putting the intellect that had made him several fortunes to work on saving his life. Possibilities raced through his mind. A man in his position had many enemies, but he couldn't think of one who'd go to such extremes. Whoever set up this operation had gone to considerable trouble. Unfortunately, the time and location of his wedding had made the papers so anyone could have anticipated his schedule.

When the limousine passed the empty church parking lot, the magnitude of this operation sank in. Somehow his huge society wedding had been canceled. Where was everyone? Had his bride been kidnapped, too?

He gritted his teeth in frustration and took a moment for his thoughts to race past the astonishing fact that not one family member had called to commiserate about his canceled marriage. His parents, Eva and Red, hadn't phoned, neither had Max or his sister-in-law, Brooke.

No matter what reason his mother had been given for the change in plans, that his mother hadn't called weighed heavily on his heart. Eva, the ultimate party planner, couldn't resist interfering—helping, she called it—in her sons' lives. That his foe could outsmart his mother chilled him more than any previous thought.

Snapping on the intercom, Ford forced his tone to normalcy. "Where are you taking me?"

"To the airport," a female voice replied, surprising him with her gender.

The rearview mirror angled downward, and he couldn't see her face. Releasing his seat belt, he slid to the other side of the car and frowned. Her exotic cheekbones and delicate tawny skin looked familiar, but he couldn't place her. Wisps of curly hair escaped her cap, and while she kept her hands steady on the wheel, the pulse in her throat beat wildly.

She wasn't as calm as she appeared. Good. He could use that to his advantage.

"In the pocket behind my seat is a pair of handcuffs." She issued instructions in a voice accustomed to giving orders. "Place them over your wrists and lock them."

In your dreams, lady.

Ford hadn't felt this helpless since Rhonda had died. Not only had he been unable to prevent her death, he lived with the failure of locating and identifying her murderer. That he'd hired the best private investigators and they'd found nothing didn't ease his need to see justice done. Being forced to face a dead end hadn't sat well with him. Neither did being forced to don handcuffs.

Seething, he swung around until his back rested on the seat with his soles placed against the rear window. Jerking his knees to his chest, then straightening his legs, he rammed his heels into the glass.

The window didn't crack. The driver didn't say a word. With a muffled curse, he repeated his kick twice more, receiving a wrenching jar to his joints for his effort. But the glass remained intact.

The handcuffs dangled tauntingly from the seat

pocket. It didn't help his temper to realize he wouldn't be leaving this vehicle a free man.

"The car's equipped with gas," she informed him, her tone casual. "Unless you put on the cuffs, I'll be forced to knock you out. The choice is yours."

"Some choice."

"The gas won't hurt," she assured him in a naggingly familiar voice, "but you'll wake up with a ferocious headache."

He straightened in his seat. "After the airport, where are you taking me?"

"We'll refuel in London before flying to Bern."

He removed his bow tie and slipped it into his pocket. "What about customs? I don't have a passport."

"I've taken care of the travel arrangements." Holding a passport to the glass partition separating them, she verified her statement. He recognized the coffee mark that had stained the cover during a bumpy flight from Saigon to Singapore.

Damn! He'd had that passport in his hands this morning. She or a cohort must have broken into his home, either while he'd caught a two-hour nap or during his shower. Only a pro could have successfully sneaked past his security system. As his chance to escape lessened, his frustration soared. The lack of answers irritated him almost as much as his lack of control over the situation. If only he knew who and why someone wanted him. And why had the wedding been called off?

Lindsay was the obvious suspect. His bride was in charge of the wedding. She had the phone numbers of guests, caterers and flower shops, but he couldn't

picture her canceling the wedding. She had nothing
to gain from his kidnapping.

When his kidnapper drove past New Orleans airport toward the private planes, his eyebrows rose a
notch. A commercial flight with other passengers offered opportunities for escape, but now that chance
would be denied him. However, there would be other
chances—even if he had to create them. He'd survived tighter spots than this one, and he wouldn't remain the victim for long or his name wasn't Ford
Braddack.

Biding his time, he took in the deserted private
fields. Few pilots would choose to depart in this thunderstorm. Unfortunately, if she gassed him, no one
would witness his body being carried aboard a plane.

He refocused his attention on the driver and used
the direct approach to learn more about his abduction.
"Why are you kidnapping me?"

"For the money," she told him without a trace of
shame.

"I'll double your fee to let me go."

She pulled off her cap and shook her head. Curly
golden hair streaked with blond and honey cascaded
past her shoulders. "I can't accept."

"Why not?" he pressed, curious what she wanted
from him. She'd captured his attention, and it wasn't
just her brazen attitude or the defiant tilt of her head.
There was something about her he should remember....

"I gave my word," she explained. "To change
sides would be dishonorable."

He groaned. Lord save him from *honorable* kid-
nappers. "Who hired you?"

"I don't know."

"What!"

The woman wasn't just a little unhinged, she was certifiable. Or she'd reached the limit of information she was willing to share. Or she was lying.

She drove slowly to the electric gate of the Executive Center, while for a moment, cutting off his ability to speak through the intercom. She spoke crisply and confidently to the guard, "NC33NI. I've baggage to unload."

He recognized the tail number of his Gulf Stream Three. The woman intended to kidnap him with his own plane! He slammed his fist into the glass, but the guard didn't appear to notice. He couldn't keep the sarcasm from his tone. "You don't know who you work for?"

She drove through the gate and glanced at him in the mirror, her eyes wary but determined. "My assignments from this client come by mail, my fee paid in cash and delivered by messenger."

Tinted windows prevented him from signaling the guard. "Where was the letter postmarked?"

"New Orleans." She held up her hand to forestall his next question. "I tried to trace the messenger, but his boss had taken a cash order with no name or return address."

He couldn't think of a way to shake her story or bribe her and wished that didn't impress him. Now was not the time to concede admiration for the enemy, but as a businessman, he knew the rarity of employee loyalty. He also appreciated the difficulty in carrying out a complex plan with such military precision.

He thumped his fingers on the armrest. "You'd risk jail time?"

"I don't think you'll report me."

She said the words with such confidence, he could only conclude her employer meant to kill him—especially since she hadn't concealed her face. Or maybe his foe wanted something from him *before* killing him. Hiding his latest alarming thoughts behind a stoic expression, he vowed to react to the slightest opportunity for escape.

"You don't remember me, do you?" Her soft question broke into his gloomy thoughts.

She tilted the mirror to reflect her face back at him. Her hair, a rich, glowing bronze-gold, tumbled carelessly down her back. Wispy bangs caressed her forehead. Tawny skin showed off generously curved lips, a straight nose and arched golden eyebrows. The defiant line of her jaw contrasted with the momentary hint of vulnerability flickering in topaz eyes emboldened with a dash of gold. Then her lids lowered, and he questioned whether the vulnerability had been there at all. He must have been mistaken.

"Have we met?" he asked, confounded by the disappointment in her expression.

"Once. At your wedding."

He shrugged. Why was his failed memory of a brief encounter five years ago important to her? Now he must really be imagining things. "I'm afraid that was a long time ago." Since then, he'd loved and lost Rhonda, had to go on alone and had to bear the knowledge that she'd been murdered without ever knowing she had a daughter. "Since then, I've met many people..."

"I thought I'd renew our acquaintance at Rhonda's funeral. But *you* never showed." Her eyes gleamed with an accusatory shimmer brighter than an avenging angel's halo.

He kept his tone calm. "I was in a coma."

"Don't joke. There's nothing funny about missing your wife's funeral," she said angrily.

"I'm telling the truth. I almost died in the avalanche." Suddenly he wanted her to believe him, although he wasn't sure why. "A rock hit me in the head. I spent several months recuperating in a hospital."

"Odd how your family claimed you were in Europe—grieving."

The driver knew a lot about his past and that should be a clue to her identity, but he still couldn't place her. She was the kind of woman he tended to notice. With her striking skin and hair, those topaz eyes and full lips, he failed to see how he could have forgotten her.

Was she a friend of Rhonda's?

If she was out for revenge, setting her straight had to be his first priority. Only his parents, brother and sister-in-law knew the truth and they'd lied to the newspapers. He kept his voice as reasonable as possible under the circumstances. "My family put out false information to protect me."

"Protect you?"

"From Rhonda's killer." His parents had feared Rhonda's murderer would return to kill him as he lay unconscious. So while he was in a coma in a New Orleans private hospital, they'd put out the word that he was still in Europe.

"No one ever found your *wife's* killer, did they?"

At the reminder of his failure to find her murderer, acid burned his stomach. He'd spent a fortune on private investigators. None had turned up a clue. It was as if the assassin had vanished, leaving him to brood with his grief.

The driver sounded as if she'd had a personal stake in Rhonda's death, a fact that contradicted his image of a hired kidnapper. More confused than ever, he closed his eyes. Suddenly the pieces clicked.

"You're Denise—Rhonda's cousin."

"Bingo."

No wonder he hadn't recognized her. Although roommates in college, Denise had never been around when he picked up Rhonda. After their marriage, he hadn't seen Denise, although his wife had often spoken to her cousin on the phone. That's why he recognized the voice; he'd taken messages.

He vaguely recalled the woman had majored in criminal justice and owned a P.I. firm. She'd never married—no wonder. He was beginning to think she had gone off the deep end.

"Just where in hell do you think you're taking me?"

"I heard you once swore to track down Rhonda's killer."

He had, but how had she come by the information? His brother wouldn't repeat such a private confession, and he didn't think Max's wife, Brooke, would either.

When he remained silent, she stared at him accusingly. "I thought you might help me."

According to Rhonda, Denise was a real loner. His wife had never mentioned mental instability or a life of crime. At the time, he hadn't pressed the issue, letting Rhonda deal with her relatives as she thought best. Now he wished he knew more. He forced himself to focus on the present and put the past aside. "Help you how?"

"Find Rhonda's killer," she said as if he were denser than a pet rock. "My normal P.I. skills usually involve tracking cheating husbands and divorcés who avoid meeting their financial obligations to their ex-wives and children, not going after killers. Besides, I don't know my way around Europe—"

"Hire a guide."

"I don't have your business or social connections."

A lot of good his money and networking had done him when he'd tried to find the killer. "I hired the best private investigators. None of them turned up a clue."

Pride and a hint of challenge entered her tone. "You should have hired me."

Chapter Two

Ford leaned forward in the seat, his eyes glinting with a savage inner chill. "You've found something?"

"Have you ever heard of the Black Rose?" Denise asked, dreading the consequences if she couldn't win him to her cause. Not even the cancellation of his wedding and kidnapping him had shaken his infamous control.

"Is the Black Rose your employer?"

She shook her head, his suggestion enough to make her eyes sting. "I loved Rhonda and I wouldn't work for her killer. In fact, my client hired me to find the Black Rose. These past six months I've kept searching for clues concerning Rhonda's death."

While the police may have forgotten the murder, Denise hadn't. The unsolved crime gnawed at her like an aching tooth. She'd considered asking Ford to hire her to investigate the murder, but he hadn't showed at Rhonda's funeral. Then she'd heard he hired three different investigating teams—naturally, the best money could buy. So she'd investigated on her own, but she hadn't had the funds to pursue a European investigation until her client hired her to solve the murder and kidnap Ford. Now she had the means to go after the killer, and she meant to put him away for good. If she had to, she'd work alone, but Ford's assistance would increase her chance of success. Her task would have been easier if she could have openly approached him with the clues she'd found and asked for his help. But her client forbid that tactic, insisting she kidnap him from his wedding before revealing what her investigation had uncovered. Since Denise had needed the funds to go after Rhonda's killer, she had to follow her client's wishes. More than anything else in the world, she wanted to bring Rhonda's killer to justice.

But the kidnapping made the complicated relationship between her and Ford more difficult. Working together would be impossible until she convinced Ford of her intentions. As Denise stepped on the brake, parking inside Norton Industries' hangar, she wondered if she could convince him to cooperate in tracking down Rhonda's killer. She glanced back at him. His polished veneer masked his fury over her kidnapping him—until she noted his fingers biting into the soft leather seat, the muscle pulsing in his jaw and the lethal iciness in his eyes. His awesome control reminded her of the power he wielded, the respect he commanded in the financial world and how very much he had loved her cousin.

"And?" he prodded.

"According to a maid at your Swiss hotel, a black rose was left on your wife's pillow. The maid threw it away without mentioning it to the gendarmes during their investigation."

"So what?"

"This is just a guess, but I think the killer left the flower as a calling card. There were two of them, by the way. One on each of your pillows."

His gaze pierced her with bold frankness. "You're suggesting we were both supposed to die in that avalanche?"

The American papers had lacked details on the skiing accident that had claimed Rhonda's life. From the reports she'd read, the couple had been skiing the same Swiss slope. Was it simply fate that Ford had survived and her cousin had not?

Denise had a hunch Ford was telling the truth when he'd claimed he'd been in a coma. The entire story had not been told. Oddly, the Swiss police report was just as deficient in facts as the news stories in the States. "You were skiing together. How did you survive the avalanche?"

In the rearview mirror, she caught the taut look of horror on Ford's rugged face and flinched. His eyelids compressed into a hard-bitten anger. Sitting back, he crossed his arms over his broad chest. Fury and pain lurked in his eyes and his lips tightened with disapproval. "Why did you cancel my wedding? What did you tell my family?"

His harsh questions rolled off her like rainwater on the limo's hood. Clients often vented their fury on her, but never did a client draw her as he did. She made herself look at him. In his hot rage, he was compelling, and her blood thrummed at the sight of all that contained power. His dark hair emphasized the grim line of his square jaw, while the muscles flexing in his neck warned her to be careful. As his searing glare struck her like a thunderbolt and she realized she'd caused that smoldering hostility, she released an unsteady sigh and faced facts. No matter how formidable he might be, no matter how extensive his financial empire, no one else had as much reason to help her.

Swallowing hard, she checked her watch. Admiring him behind bulletproof glass wasn't the same as dealing with him with only a few molecules of air between them. Suddenly the handcuffs didn't seem enough protection.

She fiddled with the gas switch, wondering if she should leave the decision to him. Even now, kidnapped and caged, he refused to answer her questions and instead, demanded answers. While she debated how much to say, she considered how incensed he would be upon awakening if she gassed him without giving him a choice. Feeling as if she held a predator at bay, she attempted to calm her jittery nerves by taking a deep breath.

"Why don't we discuss our plans on the plane?" she said.

"My plans don't include you. I'm not going anywhere until you supply answers."

His voice was so shivery-cold that despite the protective glass between them, Denise recoiled. For a moment, she saw herself through his eyes. An unprincipled private investigator. A liar. A kidnapper. But no matter his opinion, she would never forget that Rhonda had been like a sister, and she owed her, bigtime.

So did Ford. Her cousin had loved him enough to risk her health to try and bear his child. Rhonda had thought Ford could walk on water. Years ago, for two college semesters, Denise had listened to her cousin sing Ford's praises, but she'd never begrudged her the happiness she'd found. Especially since Denise and Ford had never really met. Ford had called Rhonda from the phone in the lobby of the all-female dorm, and she'd always gone downstairs to meet him, flying out of the room with a smile on her face. Denise made no special effort to meet Ford, preferring the air of mystery that had lent to his charm. But she'd trade Ford in a minute if she could have Rhonda back.

No man could live up to the romantic perfection Rhonda had spoken about—not even Ford. Damn it! Denise admonished herself. She was supposed to be on a job—not on a trip down memory lane. This time with Ford would reveal his flaws and banish the past, as well as lead them to Rhonda's killer.

As she drove into the hangar, she reached forward, her fingers on the switch that would release the gas into the passenger compartment. Hoping he wouldn't see through her bluff, she hardened her tone, "You prefer to sleep through the transfer to the plane?"

As if the gesture meant nothing, he plucked the handcuffs from the seat pocket and snapped the metal over his wrists. He moved so quickly, she lost the chance to demand he place his hands behind his back. Now it was too late.

Gulping air, she exited the car. When she opened the door, she half expected him to lunge and tackle her. A muscle pulsed in his jaw, the cords in his neck tightened above his loosened shirt collar, and there could be no mistaking the formidable menace in his stare. To her relief, he didn't attack—for which she offered a silent prayer of thanks.

He held up his manacled wrists, a patronizing curl on his lips. "You do have a key to these?"

"On the plane," she hedged, lying through omission since she had no intention of unlocking the cuffs until the plane flew past the turning-back point.

"Let's go." *One step at a time. Get him on the plane. Then deal with the consequences.*

He stomped toward the plane, no doubt hoping the pilot might come to his rescue, but the man was procuring a last-minute weather report in the Executive Center.

"Wait a sec." From the rear seat of the limo, she removed her backpack and slung it over her shoulder, leaving her hand free for his luggage—packed for his honeymoon. Thankful for the wheels that made towing the bag easy, she followed him into the plane, leaving the baggage by the door for the pilot to stow.

"This way." She led him to a padded leather chair. "Have a seat."

When she pulled another pair of handcuffs from her pocket along with a syringe, he went still. She could see him half crouched, probably debating whether to tackle her. "Don't even think it," she said. She raised the syringe without hesitation, yet wondered if she could really use it. "I'm confining your ankles around the table post only while I go to the Exec Center to bring back your pilot."

"Fine."

He eased into the seat and stretched out his feet on either side of the post. His catlike movements reminded her of a panther curling up for a nap, relaxed, but ever ready to pounce.

Watching him warily, she restrained his ankles. She

removed a gag from her pocket. "I can't have you calling for help."

He didn't protest, but his scowling lips let her know exactly how he felt about this last indignity and warned her payback time wouldn't be pleasant. But she refused to let his glare deter her.

After tying the gag, she clasped her hands behind her back to hide their shaking. She must have been crazy to agree to kidnapping him. Only her love for Rhonda gave her the courage to proceed. Still, one glance into his dangerous eyes confirmed he would not soon forget or forgive what she'd done.

Her stomach churned with anxiety as she recalled Ford had made his fortune, not inherited it. His ruthlessness was feared by his competitors. Even his wife had been awed by him. And Denise had had the temerity to kidnap him from his wedding, handcuff and gag him aboard his own plane. He might be sitting helpless before her, but she was shaking so hard, she had to fight the urge to beg forgiveness.

She fled the plane and his accusing stare as fast as her legs would take her. On the way to fetch the pilot, she wiped her fingerprints off the syringe, broke the needle and tossed it into the glove compartment of the limo, where later one of her employees could see to its safe disposal.

She found the pilot and chatted with him, mentioning how anxious Mr. Braddack was to take off. Her hint worked, and for once luck was with her as the wind died and the rain ceased falling. After stowing their bags, the unsuspecting pilot climbed into the cockpit and began his preflight check.

When the jet's engines revved to life, Denise, trying to calm her speeding heart, returned to Ford. As she untied the gag, the scent of his spicy cologne assailed her. Her fingers itched to smooth a stray strand of hair off his forehead. "I'll unlock your ankles in a minute."

Thick eyebrows raised, he cocked his head to the side. "What about my wrists?"

"I'll be happy to remove those once we pass the halfway point."

"And *then* what's to keep me from wringing your neck?" The violence of his statement contrasted vividly with his calm. His eyes were distant and hard. He used the same unemotional voice one might use to discuss the weather, his icy, controlled tone making him all the more menacing.

"Is that what happened to Rhonda?" she countered, resisting a shiver. "Did you leave black roses on the pillows, imitating—"

His eyes glittered like sapphires. His jaw clenched. "You know damned well *I* didn't kill her." Despite her accusation, he spoke coolly, keeping his voice low, almost a growl.

At the threat in his tone, her stomach twisted into an icy knot. He might not be shouting and lunging at her, but she couldn't mistake the coiled power in the set of his shoulders.

Despite the dangerous jut of his jaw, she still saved a soft spot in her heart for Ford. Yet she couldn't forget her last phone conversation with her cousin, before Rhonda had taken that fatal trip to Switzerland.

"Ford's lost all patience with me," Rhonda had admitted.

"What do you mean?" Denise had expected Rhonda to tell her about some silly marital quarrel.

"He's forbidden me to attempt another pregnancy."

Rhonda's inability to conceive had been the source of many an argument between the pair. Ford didn't want his wife to go through any more grief in hopes of conceiving a child. But dedicated to giving her husband an heir, Rhonda had doggedly refused to accept defeat.

Denise had never forgotten the ominous emphasis Rhonda had given to *forbidden,* as if Ford's command was law, neither questioned nor amended. And the sorrow in her cousin's tone had carried the implication of great failure, which had shocked Denise, who considered Rhonda a roaring success.

She had difficulty comprehending her cousin's obsession with having children. Still, she understood impossible dreams, and clearly, the problem was affecting their marriage.

Rhonda had sobbed into the phone. "This trip is supposed to put the romance back into our lives. I don't dare disappoint him."

"Come on, it can't be that bad. This is Ford Braddack we're talking about, remember? He treats you like spun glass."

"That's the problem. He won't talk to me about his problems. He's so tense. He never relaxes anymore. I think we've forgotten how to have fun, and I'm so afraid I've lost his love."

"Not possible. Everyone loves you."

Less than a week after Rhonda's phone call, the avalanche struck down her cousin. While Ford had presumably remained in Switzerland, Rhonda arrived in New Orleans. In a coffin.

Now her cousin's husband sat across from her, clearly angrier than a stinging hornet. Her mouth went dry. She distracted herself by unlocking his ankles, then strapped herself into her seat.

In the space of the breath it took to fasten the belt, Ford pounced. He vaulted over the table, landed astride her lap, seized her by the neck with his manacled hands. As the plane taxied down the runway through the clearing skies, his strong thighs pinned her to the seat. His fingers flexed lightly but threateningly on her throat. His touch, though fierce, applied the most minimal of pressure.

While the storm's rage had spent itself and the takeoff was smooth, the fury inside Ford brewed cold and fierce. Up close, she watched his irises deepen to a steely blue. Anguish and violence warred in the depths of his eyes, surging toward her in pulsing waves. She fought her urge to test her skill against his strength by throwing him to the plane's floor.

She wasn't the vulnerable one here—at least not physically. Her hands were free. But to overcome his superior strength, she'd have to hurt him badly. With well-placed blows to groin, nose and temple, she could escape the threatening fingers on her throat. But such actions would damage his pride, and he didn't deserve humiliation. She had no wish to embarrass him, and she couldn't bring herself to hurt him further—not after what he'd already suffered. Besides, she couldn't risk injuring him when she still hoped to convince him to help her find Rhonda's killer.

"What are you doing?" Her voice vibrated as she

released the seat belt and heaved up, pushing and straining in the hopes of getting him off her without injuring him. His weight, combined with the plane's acceleration, pressed her deeper into the seat. "If you have the crazy idea I'm going to—"

"Unlock these handcuffs. Then we'll talk."

Just as she suspected, she couldn't budge him and ceased struggling. After hazarding one long uneasy glance at him, she ducked her head, before he read more in her eyes than she wanted him to see. She might not be in jeopardy of strangulation, but there were other kinds of physical danger.

His hot breath ruffled her hair. His nearness caused her pulse to race and her stomach to lurch in an unfamiliar way that had nothing to do with the plane's takeoff.

Her heart hammered stupidly, and she clenched her hands stiffly at her sides. "Calm down, Ford."

"It's too late for that."

She licked her bottom lip and wished she hadn't. While he stared at her mouth, she risked another peek into his eyes, and trembled at the crazy, hard edge to them. He wasn't bluffing. His banked temper had erupted. Only his strong-willed control kept him from snapping her neck and she questioned her ability to dislodge him.

The time for force was over.

"Get off me, and I'll unlock the handcuffs." She had to bite her tongue from adding, *please.*

"No."

She frowned. "No?"

"Unlock me," he demanded, "*then* I'll let you go."

She tilted her head back and allowed a tiny smile to curve her lip. "I'm afraid that's impossible."

"Why?"

"Because the key's in my back pocket," she told him, unable to keep amusement from her tone. His fierce expression lightened with comprehension. With the plane in flight, the force of acceleration eased, but while he pressed her into the seat, she couldn't possibly reach the key. "Now, let go of me."

"Put your arms around my neck," he ordered, ignoring her demand.

"What's your point?" When she'd considered whether to take this assignment, she'd imagined many scenarios between her and Ford—but never one like this! She hadn't expected to be so close to him, and the reality surpassed her most vivid imagination. He was larger and stronger than she'd have guessed, but it was all that energy focused on her that set her nerves flaming.

His eyes gleamed, indicating she'd lost control of the conversation. She'd underestimated him, and he'd quickly turned the situation to his advantage. While she couldn't guess what he had in mind, she suspected she wouldn't like it. She clenched her thighs tight. She'd grown careless. Now she'd pay for her mistake.

"I'll feel safer with your hands occupied."

"Safer?" She felt like a parrot, repeating his words, but she couldn't help herself. She was too aware of the hard strength of him. With his chest so close to her face, his weight straddling her lap, her brain had gone on strike.

"While you lift yourself off the seat, your hands won't be free to strike."

"But the key—"

"*I'll* retrieve the key."

Oh, God. He meant to... His hand would..."I don't think—"

"Do it." His voice whipped her with the lash of command.

She clamped her lips hard. If she refused to comply, he could pin her in the seat until they reached Europe.

Reluctantly, she wound her arms around his neck. His flesh was hot, firm, and his silky hair caressed her skin. Beneath her forearms, his shoulders tensed, bracing as she gingerly pulled herself upward.

The handcuffs jangled as he dropped both hands to her hip and reached around to her pocket. "Lean forward," he ordered.

She complied, gnashing her molars and foolishly wishing she possessed the svelte lines of the women he usually dated instead of the lush hips of a gypsy. The handcuffs made him awkward, and his hand roved across her bottom for an unusually long time, sending a warming shiver through her. A hot ache grew in the back of her throat and her pulse pounded. Her breasts squashed against his chest.

In her adolescent dreams, she'd envisioned hot kisses. Not in her wildest fantasies had she considered a man first caressing her backside, and she managed to resist the urge to squirm only by holding her breath.

Wild with impatience at his fumbling, she muttered, "Oh, for heaven's sake. Can't you find it?"

"Find what?" he said tightly.

"The key."

"Lady, I haven't even found the pocket."

"Oh." Mortified at his insinuation that her rear was so large, she pressed her lips together, determined not to utter another sound.

"You sure the key is there?" he asked, as if suspecting she enjoyed the forced intimacy.

Yeah, right. She was lying so he could fondle her. She wasn't that hard up for a man's touch. Just when she thought she couldn't bear another second, his fingers dived deeper.

"Got it!"

He stood, breaking her hold. She plopped back into the seat, willing back a blush, trembling and hoping he didn't notice. Running a hand through her curls, she glared at him. "I'm allowing you to free yourself—"

"Is that so?" His hand with the key paused over the lock while he eyed her skeptically.

"To help me find the Black Rose," she continued as if he hadn't interrupted.

"Suppose I don't want to find your Black Rose? What if I order *my* pilot to turn *my* plane around and report you to the authorities?"

If he was trying to bully her, his tactic wouldn't work. "I can kick the key out of your hand from here. I can't guarantee where it'll land, but I assure you, I'll be the one who finds it."

"Meaning?"

She shrugged, matching him stare for stare. "Meaning, I don't go down easy. But I didn't bring you along for a punching bag."

"Glad to hear it."

"I'd hoped you'd cooperate." She held her breath,

waiting to see what he'd do. Would his curiosity and intelligence win out over his anger?

He closed his fingers around the key so tightly the skin across his knuckles stretched taut. He took the opposite seat without unlocking the handcuffs, his face inscrutable, his mouth hard. "It's time you explained."

"I'll tell you what I can."

"You'll tell me everything."

When pigs fly. She didn't argue. But she didn't agree, either. "What do you want to know?"

"Start with what you told my bride-to-be, my family and my wedding guests."

"I informed them you canceled the wedding. I didn't give a reason."

"My mother would never buy that flimsy story."

"She didn't."

He leaned forward, his elbows on his knees, listening with a rigidity that was almost frightening. A tension vibrated between them—a tension that made her feel like a cornered rabbit about to be bagged for supper.

Denise took a deep breath and exhaled slowly. "I told your mother that I'd been working for you since Rhonda's death and I'd uncovered a clue that you intended to pursue immediately. That your bride didn't want the wedding delayed, and so you called it off."

He drummed his fingers on the table. "Go on."

Wishing she knew the thoughts behind the unfathomable expression he wore, she forced out the rest. "I asked your mother to arrange for the plane and pilot to fly out today."

His eyebrows knitted in a frown. "She must have thought your request unusual."

As the plane rose, her ears popped. "She didn't appear suspicious. After I told her about the Black Rose, Eva agreed to contact your pilot. She also volunteered to inform Max of your change in plans, so I never spoke to your brother."

His eyes bored into hers. "And my bride? What did you say to her?"

She thought it odd and significant he'd taken so long to ask about Lindsay Betancourt. She stared out the window. The sun peeked out from behind a sky clotted with clouds. Perhaps they could put the stormy weather behind them. Peering into a fat mattress of clouds, she gathered her thoughts. She'd dreaded this moment ever since his fiancée had happily agreed to take the payoff. It seemed far-fetched that Lindsay would give up a man like Ford, but perhaps dreams of stardom were more attainable than Denise's chances of finding Rhonda's murderer.

Although she didn't know him well, Ford was obviously a man of deep feelings, and for his bride to callously leave him would hurt worse than a punch in the gut. She searched for the right words to soften the blow. But the self-imposed task was impossible.

As the plane leveled, she picked out a spot beside his ear and focused there, speaking past the tightness in her throat. "I offered Lindsay money to leave you."

"And she took it," he finished. "If she wanted money, she would have gotten more by staying. So why would she go?"

His imperturbability surprised her. She'd expected

icy denial. Instead, he appeared more analytical than hurt, infuriated or indignant. His temper had evaporated as if it had never been, and his cool control made telling the rest a bit easier.

"Lindsay wants to be an actress. For her, the money is a way to achieve her dream."

"Apparently the role of wife wasn't enough," he said thoughtfully, as if he'd known Lindsay's affection for him hadn't been deep. But if he had known, why had he asked her to marry him? Could he have fallen head over heels in love with his bride, thinking she'd learn to love him? If so, he wasn't showing much disappointment.

When she remained silent, he rubbed the handcuff key between his fingers. "I suppose I should thank your client."

"Thank?"

He'd astonished her back to parroting his words again. Why wasn't he hurt? Or angry? Or speaking in that ultracold voice that indicated real fury?

"I ought to let you stew in your guilt. But I never felt for Lindsay what I did for Rhonda." He bowed his head, the key in his hand seemingly forgotten. "I should have known better."

At his simple words, her heart went out to him. She only hoped encouraging him to search for Rhonda's killer would ease the grief that seemed a permanent part of him. "Who do you think hired me?"

At her question, he jerked back in his seat and seemed to look inward, giving her query his full attention. A ray of sunlight broke through the clouds, brightening the cabin. The fasten-your-seat-belt lights went off.

Finally, he spoke carefully as if weighing how much to reveal. "Martin Crewsdale, my partner, warned me repeatedly against marrying Lindsay."

"You think your partner hired me?"

"Martin is rather conservative. While I tend to acquisitions and troubleshooting, Martin runs the day-to-day operations of Norton Industries. Despite our partnership and his disapproval of Lindsay, I doubt he'd resort to kidnapping."

"Was Martin your only associate who disapproved of Miss Betancourt?"

"That list is quite long. My secretary, several friends, even my pilot made their objections clear. Actually, I can't think of anyone who approved of the marriage." He paused for a moment as if startled by the revelation, as if he rarely considered the opinions of friends before making personal decisions. "In addition, there are several wealthy women who aren't above paying off the competition. But I suspect someone closer to me orchestrated this plan."

She sucked in her breath. "You mean, family?"

He shrugged. "Right now, I'm more interested in finding Rhonda's murderer. Tell me about the Black Rose."

Good. She'd snagged his attention. Cooperation would follow. She projected her voice above the steady drone of the airplane's engines. "The black flowers aren't my only clue. But let me explain the ground I've already covered so you understand why this clue is vital to my investigation." She paused, putting her thoughts in order. "Dr. Henschel—"

"Died too easy," he interrupted. His voice cracked like a whiplash. He closed his jaw so tightly, she heard his teeth snap. Ford's fists clenched and his eyes smoldered with fury and glazed with regret.

Denise didn't blame him for his outrage. Ford was on the board of directors at the Kine Fertility Clinic. He and her cousin had gone to Dr. Henschel asking for help to have a child. A mix-up had led to disaster when Rhonda's egg had been implanted in another woman.

Rhonda had miscarried, unaware that another woman, Nicole, had given birth to Rhonda's biological daughter, Skye. Two months after the baby's birth, Nicole and her husband were killed in a car accident, and Nicole's sister, Brooke Evans, raised Skye. Six years later when Brooke discovered Skye was not Nicole's, Dr. Henschel had been caught trying to save his career by covering up the switched embryos—but not before he'd hired an assassin to murder Rhonda. The doctor committed suicide in jail, leaving few clues to identify Rhonda's assassin.

Ford's pain renewed her determination to find the killer. "I searched Henschel's financial records."

"My people went through those records, too. His transactions were always in cash, and therefore, untraceable."

"That's almost correct. But Henschel wired two substantial cash deposits to a Swiss bank—one about a week before your wife's death, one the day after. That's why we're flying to Bern."

She didn't spell out the implications. From the slight lift of his eyebrows, Ford understood the significance of the timing of Dr. Henschel's financial transactions. A large financial transfer from Dr. Henschel to a Swiss bank one week before Rhonda's death might be coincidence. But a second payment, the day after her death couldn't be ignored. The timing smelled of a payoff.

Unlocking the cuffs, he tossed them onto the table. "Go on."

Grateful she no longer needed to restrain him, the tension eased from the rigid muscles of her neck and shoulders. Until now, she hadn't realized how much she'd counted on Ford's help. "Swiss banks are not in the habit of divulging their customers' names. Your influence might turn up a lead."

He nodded. "I have a few friends overseas. I'll make some calls from the plane. Perhaps we might have answers when we arrive. What else do you have?"

"Grendal Archer, the maid who threw away the black flowers, disappeared right after she failed to mention the roses to the police. But she did tell another maid, my informant. Suspicious, yes? My informant thinks Grendal will give us a description of the Black Rose. And I have Grendal's new address."

"That's more than my investigators turned up."

"I told you that you should have hired me."

"Really?"

"There's one more thing you should know." Her fingers twisted in her lap. She'd wrestled with the knowledge for weeks, unable to turn up any solid evidence. "I've heard rumors the Black Rose may be more than a common criminal."

"What do you mean?"

"The Black Rose is a professional assassin. Even

worse, instinct tells me we're heading into danger.''
She looked him straight in the eyes. ''And I have very
good instincts.''

Chapter Three

They zoomed through customs due to the efficiency of the Swiss. Outside, the crisp air revived Denise from nagging jet lag. More accustomed to traveling, Ford had changed clothes and slept on the plane, and he now looked awake and eager.

A gleaming black Rolls Royce, accompanied by a short, bald man who spoke in an articulate British accent, met them at the airport. He wore a burgundy belted jacket over creamy flannel trousers. A flowered ascot looped casually around his scrawny neck drooped as he leaned heavily on a cane. "Bruce Willowby, British embassy." After the rest of the introductions, he gestured for them to sit in the rear of his car. "Put their luggage in the boot," Ambassador Willowby instructed the pilot, who would stay behind to ready the plane for their trip home.

As if accustomed to foreign diplomats waiting on his beck and call, Ford gave the driver an address that Denise recognized as the same Swiss hotel where he'd stayed with Rhonda. Contacting the English embassy instead of the American diplomats might be a shrewd move if anyone was interested in their mission, but for the assassin to already know they pursued him seemed unlikely. Still, she couldn't help looking over her shoulder. She saw only charming steep-roofed chalets amid wildflowers and grazing cattle.

Ford turned to Willowby and assessed him coolly. "You have the information I requested?"

As promised, Ford had called ahead from the plane, requesting details on Dr. Henschel's suspicious wire transfers to the Swiss bank. In addition, he'd made hotel reservations, and arranged for a rental car to be waiting at the hotel.

Willowby pursed thin lips. "The Swiss are notoriously reticent about sharing the particulars of private transactions. We have asked for their cooperation through diplomatic channels. However, you might have more success on your own."

Denise stared into the side mirror. A car behind them copied their every turn. The hair on her nape stood on end, sending goose bumps over her flesh. Refusing to let the men's conversation distract her, she memorized the license-plate number and noted the driver's features.

Nonchalantly, Ford crossed an ankle over his knee as if he'd expected Willowby's news. "I see."

Denise didn't see at all. What "private channels" were they talking about? She'd question Ford later. After all, this was why she'd wanted his help—for his connections to Europe's rich, influential and famous. She'd brought him along to do his thing, now she'd best sit back and let him do it.

"You have names for me?" Ford asked.

Willowby handed him a slip of paper and two gold-embossed invitations on creamy paper. "The embassy is hosting a party tonight. I suggest you speak to this banker."

Without looking at the name, Ford placed the paper in his pocket. "Thank you."

Willowby cleared his throat. "There's another matter of some importance."

At the edge in the diplomat's tone, Denise took her gaze off her first view of the snow-capped Alps and darted her eyes back to the side-view mirror. "We're being followed."

"Are you sure?" Ford turned to look over his shoulder.

At his question, she raised her eyebrows. "Quite sure."

"Not to worry," Willowby murmured. "I took the precaution of bringing along additional protection. You may need it. In fact, if you carry through with your plans, I suggest you hire a professional."

Ford frowned. "Why?"

"The Black Rose?" Denise guessed.

"Very good. That's a sharp woman you've got there."

Although he had complimented her, Denise hated being talked about as if she weren't present. But now was not the time to demand equal treatment. They needed information and Willowby seemed uneasy about imparting what he knew.

The diplomat's upper lip broke into a sweat. "This Black Rose is best left alone. MI5 information on him is scanty. You can't bring your wife back, Mr. Braddack. Perhaps you should go home before you—"

Ford crossed his arms over his chest. "No."

"Please tell us what you can," Denise suggested.

"I don't have much to offer. The Black Rose is a deadly assassin. He could be Middle-Eastern, Asian, or even European or American. We simply don't know. No one who sees his face is left alive to identify him."

Ford's expression remained unreadable. "How long has this guy been operating?"

"We suspect twelve to fifteen years."

"How is he contacted?" Denise asked.

"Could be through the post, by exchanging messages at a bookstall or through the Internet. Sorry, we don't know. After he accepts a contract, he leaves a black rose on the mark's pillow. None of his victims have survived."

Ford had. Denise and Ford exchanged a long look, and he shook his head slightly, signaling her to remain silent.

"Is there more?"

Willowby tapped his cane against his shoe. "MI5 suspects that during the past year, the Black Rose has assassinated several African leaders, one Middle Eastern despot and two members of the Chinese underworld. He prefers a long-range rifle with a silencer, but is willing to make a death appear accidental if necessary."

Ford considered their new information. "My wife and I hardly fit in with such elite targets."

"If the money is right, the Black Rose will accept any contract. Some assassins are motivated by ego and take only the most prestigious hits. The Black Rose is motivated by money. He's careful, a pro, and he's damn good at his job."

The English diplomat's speech ended when they arrived at the hotel. As Willowby waved goodbye and a bellhop carried their luggage from the car, Denise looked around. She'd expected something grandiose, more ornate—not this picture-perfect elegance. The inn perched in a hollow of smooth grassland. It was early afternoon and with the Alps in the distance amid bright sunlight, the majestic setting had a grace and beauty lovelier than she could have imagined. Terraces sloped to gardens, and gardens to a deep blue lake.

She envisioned Rhonda here, basking in Swiss proficiency, dining on gourmet delicacies, pampered by the gracious staff. After her cousin and Ford married, Rhonda spent her time heading charity functions in designer gowns while Denise slaved to make her P.I. firm a success. After a few years gathering evidence on cheating husbands for their suspicious wives, Denise's trust in the male species was about as flimsy as her clients' failing marriages.

Although Rhonda and Denise had traveled in different social circles, they frequently spoke on the phone and just the two of them met for lunch at least once a month. Denise had never been good at small talk, flirting or gossiping, which would have kept her from fitting in with Rhonda's country-club set. Frankly, Ford and Rhonda's friends intimidated her. Besides, she'd been busy with her firm, trying to stay in business. She had neither the time nor the money to shop for the clothes needed to fit into their crowd. Despite numerous invitations, Denise had kept her distance from the couple and their upper-class crowd so as not to embarrass them.

The ambience of the Swiss luxury hotel might be welcoming, but Denise's nerves jangled. Ford sauntered through the lobby with the self-assurance of a man belonging to the same exclusive and privileged crowd that made her so uncomfortable.

A little more than half a year ago, he and Rhonda had come to this hotel to renew their romance. Instead, he'd lost his wife forever. How could he stand to return?

Ford stared at her with somber curiosity. "What's wrong?"

"I was just converting kilometers to miles and figuring how long it would take to drive to Grendal's address," she lied. "What time is the embassy party?"

"Seven."

The uniformed bellman led them through the silent lobby, over a covered walkway, and to a private bungalow out back. She was about to protest that she needed her own quarters, but as if reading her mind, Ford put his finger to his lips.

He tipped the bellman, who left them alone in a chalet full of antiques. A high ceiling and huge glass windows overlooked a wraparound deck. Striding to the massive stone fireplace that dominated the open kitchen and living area, she closed the drapes and waited for Ford's explanation.

He gestured up a staircase. "There are two bedrooms. If we hire additional protection, it'll be easier to keep us safe if we remain together."

He'd spoken in a businesslike tone, and she attempted to match his insouciant air. "Fine. I thought I'd take a fast shower, then drive out to Grendal's home. I'll meet you back here after the embassy party and we'll compare notes.''

"No."

Her head jerked up and their gazes locked. In his navy sport coat and khaki pants, he possessed the carefree ease of a corporate president accustomed to giving orders that would be obeyed without dissent. Just the angle of his head suggested he expected her to agree. But she wasn't his employee or even his client, and no matter how much he fascinated her, she refused to let him order her around.

She held his stare. "Excuse me?"

"First of all, you didn't sleep on the plane, and tired people make mistakes. Second, we need to arrange protection before we go anywhere. Third, Grendal's description of the Black Rose can wait until tomorrow. And fourth, I want you at the embassy party with me. I'd like your opinion of our contact."

"I'm not tired. I couldn't possibly sleep until it's dark. Besides, I'm sure your assessment of a banker would be more accurate than mine. Furthermore the assassin can't possibly know I'm tracking him down. You go ahead and arrange protection. I have this feeling I need to talk to Grendal before she runs again."

"Another day won't make a difference."

Her feeling about reaching Grendal immediately was a strong one. She wouldn't allow Ford to talk her out of following her hunch. "I have nothing to wear to a party. Why don't you go without me?"

He didn't contradict her but picked up the phone, dialed and murmured a few sentences in French. "Answer their questions about sizes, and they'll send appropriate attire."

She'd order the clothes, but that didn't mean she'd go with him. While appreciative that he left the room while she gave her size over the phone, she still didn't like how he'd tried to rearrange and control her schedule.

The idea of attending a fancy party caused her stomach to roil with dread. The thought of accompanying Ford actually made her more nervous than the possibility of facing the Black Rose.

Parties required small talk and dancing. She'd never mastered the art of chatting with strangers; dancing she couldn't do at all. Her teenage years were a social failure from which she'd never recovered. She'd preferred to be left alone rather than face the humiliation of never knowing what to say. A complete social klutz, she couldn't accompany and embarrass a man accustomed to escorting debutantes.

Besides, she had work to do. She hadn't flown all this way to attend some damn fancy party and finesse information out of a Swiss banker, when Ford could more than adequately take care of it. Marching upstairs to unpack and shower, she formed a plan.

Her room had an antique dresser and a four-poster bed decorated with a blue, green and pink patchwork quilt. Matching curtains over the windows gave the chamber a homey feel. The connecting marble bath was pure sybaritic luxury. Potpourri scented the air with the fragrance of wildflowers. Thick terry towels embroidered with the inn's initials hung over towel heaters. At the sight of the whirlpool tub and the basket of inviting bath oils, she yearned for a long, hot soak. Instead, she settled for a shower and used the phone by her bed to call a taxi.

Leaving Ford a note on her pillow, she sneaked downstairs, hoping he wouldn't hear her from his room. She didn't want to admit to him she often worked on a hunch. And her dislike of parties was none of his business.

She escaped to the lobby and headed toward the door. A hand clamped down on her shoulder. With a gasp, she whirled to find Ford looming over her.

"Going somewhere?" he asked with a sardonic arch of his eyebrow.

She lifted her chin. "You don't own me."

He shook his head, his eyes twinkling, and she realized not only had he anticipated her slipping away, he wasn't angry about it. Not what she'd expected. Go figure. The man was full of surprises, some of them even pleasant.

Taking her elbow, he led her outside toward a white Volvo. He commandeered the driver's seat, still without one word of rebuke. "There's a map in the glove compartment. Let's go find Grendal Archer."

An hour later, after passing a handful of farms and verdant, undulating countryside, he pulled into a tiny mountain village, past a thriving vegetable and flower market. Goats, chickens and cows roamed the streets. The fresh scent of baled hay and grass mixed with cow manure.

Consulting the map, she directed Ford past the prosperous old town down a dirt lane. Steep-roofed cottages decorated the mountainside. In the valley, he pulled up to a broad box farmhouse, with a deep-curving roof that sloped nearly to the ground.

Her neck prickled. "Something's wrong."

"What?"

"I'm not sure. It's too quiet." She eased her hand into her backpack and pulled out her pistol.

"How'd you sneak that weapon past customs?"

She shrugged. "I guessed the inspectors wouldn't think a woman with you would carry anything more dangerous in her bag than a tube of lipstick."

She expected Ford to scold her and tensed.

"You wouldn't happen to have another weapon, would you?"

"Do you know how to use one?"

"Yes."

After giving him a hard look and realizing he meant what he said, she reached into her pack and handed him a second gun. "It's loaded but on safety. You've got nine rounds. Here's another clip."

"Thanks."

When he took the gun from her, their fingers touched and his heat zinged up her arm. Alarmed he could affect her with just a touch, she jerked back. Now was not the time for distractions.

Smoke curled lazily from the chimney, but no one came outside. In an isolated town like this, visitors must be rare, but not so much as a curtain twitched to indicate anyone eyeing them curiously.

"Now what?" Ford asked, for once willing to follow her lead.

While her blood heated in anticipation of a fight or flight, she couldn't help sparing a thought for Ford's uncommon good sense. Hunting for a witness was more her area of expertise than his, and he recognized that.

"I'll knock on the front door."

"You want me to cover you or go around back?" he asked before she could suggest either option.

She considered the alternatives. "If Grendal answers the door and everything appears normal, then there's no reason you can't come inside with me. But if I don't signal, cover me until I'm in—then go around back."

"Got it."

After carefully arranging the backpack to hang from her shoulder, she placed her hand, holding the gun, inside the pack. If all was normal, she needn't frighten Grendal. But if necessary, she could shoot through the thin material. Opening the car door, she slipped out.

"Be careful," Ford warned.

"Roger that," she replied, warmed by his concern.

She knocked on the door, feeling exposed and vulnerable. Yet even an expert marksman couldn't pick her off from as far away as the nearest likely hiding spot. In front of the farmhouse, the meadow extended for over three miles before meeting a fence or tree.

When no one answered, she knocked harder. The door creaked open from the force of her pounding. "Hello. Anyone home?"

No one responded. Not even a dog barked.

Freeing her gun from the pack, she stepped over the threshold, and immediately crouched to one side. The scent of lemon floor wax lingered with the stink of stale smoke. She waited for her eyes to adjust to the relative darkness and took her bearings. Shutters barred the windows, and drapes had been pulled to keep out light that might have seeped through the cracks. The house didn't appear large. She stood in the gloomy great room, guessing perhaps two or three bedrooms were in back.

"Hello. Grendal?"

Gripped by tension, Denise proceeded into the smoky room. She circled, holding the gun before her with both hands. Empty.

"Denise," Ford called from outside. "I'm coming in the front door."

"Okay." He'd changed the plan with a take-control decisiveness she'd come to expect, but she was grateful not only for his company, but for the verbal warning. The silent house with its murky shadows multiplied her sense of danger. A few embers burned in the fireplace, but there was no other sign of life.

Ford ducked to enter the low-slung doorway. "Are you all right?"

"Just peachy. No sign of anyone. I'll check the bedrooms." A spike of adrenaline rattled her nerves. "My neck itches."

"Why don't you go on out and stand guard. I'll check the rest," he suggested.

"We'll go together. Just remember, my instincts are screaming—"

"I know. You have good instincts."

She didn't crack a grin at his attempt at humor. Stealing down the hall, she broached the new areas quietly, carefully. The first bedroom was empty. So was the second.

On the bed in the third room, someone or something huddled beside the blankets. She pointed the gun at the unmoving lump while Ford opened the partially pulled drapes. Light filtered through the shutter onto a body.

"Grendal?" she guessed, a sinking feeling in her gut at the knowledge the woman was dead.

Dark brown blotches stained the white sheets. Blood. A bullet hole in her forehead matched one in the shutters. Grendal stared at the ceiling, wide-eyed. Denise's chest tightened with horror so fierce it hurt. Moisture blurred her eyes, and she quickly turned her back to rein in her runaway emotions.

You're a P.I. Think like one.

Denise hadn't seen many dead bodies, but this one didn't appear too stiff. She guessed they'd missed the killing by perhaps just an hour or two.

If only they'd arrived sooner, maybe they could have saved her. But if they'd arrived sooner, the assassin might have killed Ford and Denise just as efficiently, just as indifferently.

She glanced over at Grendal's body. Did she have parents who would mourn her? Children who would cry themselves to sleep at night?

What kind of person could do such a thing? And for a living? A chill invaded her bones and she fought the impulse to run and hide.

Ford plucked a tissue from a box, pulled the blanket over Grendal's face without touching the material and thrust the tissue in his pocket. "He shot her while she pulled the drapes."

"Ford, look." Denise pointed to the bedding. Across a lacy white pillow lay a single black rose petal. "She could have thrown away the rest of the flower."

"We've seen enough," Ford insisted. "Let's get out of here."

Once on the road, he tried to call the police on his cellular phone. The mountains blocked the satellite, and he couldn't get through.

"I feel responsible for that poor woman's death," he said. "Somehow, the Black Rose knew we were coming." His palm slammed the steering wheel. "How?"

Wearily, she ran her fingers through her hair. "Lots of ways. The pilot filed a flight plan. There could have been a leak at the embassy. Or someone at customs might have reported us coming into the country. Then closer to home, my employees knew my plans. You called your partner and parents from the plane."

He shook his head.

"What?"

"Martin and I have been partners for years. He's so conservative with the company finances he could work for the IRS. He's even tight-lipped when he drinks. He clears every news release with our attorneys, so he's not exactly the type to go blabbing sensitive information."

"There's your family. They could have let something slip."

"Not a chance. My parents are part of the New Orleans social set and know how fast gossip travels. When I was in that coma, no one even guessed. Mom can keep a secret. And Red—that's my dad—is one of the most closemouthed men I know."

"Someone slipped or was overheard. How else would the Black Rose know we are here?"

"Even if the assassin knew we were in Switzer-

land," he said, "how could he have known we were
going to see Grendal?"

"I don't know. Maybe he learned about her the
same way I did, through another hotel employee."
She paused, trying to banish the image of those sight-
less eyes staring at the ceiling, eyes that would never
look on the beautiful Swiss countryside again. "I
think we should report her death through an anony-
mous phone call. We can't afford to have our names
in a police report."

"Agreed. I'll call from the hotel lobby when we
get back. And I'm hiring a few bodyguards to protect
us for the rest of our stay."

They returned to the hotel with time enough for her
to bathe and attempt to force Grendal's death from
her mind. Emotionally exhausted, she sank into the
poofy-white goose-down mattress which folded
around her.

In spite of the comfort, she had trouble falling
asleep, still unnerved by the pale corpse on the pris-
tine white sheets. Had her death been their fault?
Would the Black Rose have killed the woman if Denise had stayed in Louisiana?

Her mind raced about what to do next. Checking
every flower market in Bern in hopes of finding someone who sold black roses seemed futile. Her eyes
closed. Perhaps Ford's banking contacts would di-
vulge hard information.

At a knock on her door, her eyes sprang open. The
dim light of the setting sun indicated she'd fallen
asleep. She drew the covers to her chin. "Come in."

Without glancing her way, Ford carried a variety

of boxes into her room and set them on the dresser. "Can you be ready in an hour?"

"Sure," she answered, then cursed under her breath. She'd forgotten to pretend she was ill. Ford had a way of sneaking up on her and arranging her time to dovetail with his plans. Before she could think of another excuse to avoid the party, Ford had departed and shut her door.

Another man might have looked at her, his eyes sparkling as he imagined her naked under the sheets. Ford hadn't turned his head. That he remained indifferent annoyed her.

Yet as she recalled how they'd worked together as a team this afternoon, her irritation evaporated. She'd known him capable of leadership, but he'd surprised her by following her suggestions without asking questions. On some level, he trusted her ability. Amazed by this insight into his personality, she suddenly wanted to force him to notice her as a woman. Perhaps the party would help erase the chilling image of Grendal's death.

Suddenly eager to check out the boxes, she flung off the covers and set about fixing herself up to meet a Swiss banker—or so she told herself. Exactly one hour later, she swept downstairs.

His eyes rounded. "Wow!"

Standing in the living room dressed in his tuxedo, Ford looked his normal elegant self. With his dark hair neatly combed, his blue eyes sparkled as he gazed at her with obvious approval. "You're exquisite. I'll have to fight men off to dance with you."

His sincere admiration, combined with the formfitting gold-sequined gown, gave her the courage to ad-

mit her social inexperience. She felt like a fool, but
better to confess her deficiency in private than later,
amid strangers. "I don't dance."

"All the better. I can keep you to myself for the
evening."

He sounded as if he meant it, but she didn't believe
him. His gallant manners saved her from additional
awkward explanations and she was grateful.

She bit her lip nervously. "Ford, I'm not good at
parties."

He must have heard the quiver of panic in her voice
because he stopped and pivoted. "What do you
mean?"

She shrugged and noted that his eyes never dropped
from hers to her low-cut bodice. Finding a man more
concerned with her opinions than how she filled out
her dress infused her with additional courage. "Small
talk eludes me. I can never think of anything to say."

"You're disconcerted over a party?" To his credit,
his attitude was more astonishment than condescen-
sion, so she didn't hold the smile twitching at his lips
against him. "Is this the same woman who canceled
my wedding, kidnapped me, then convinced me to
track down an international assassin?"

"Social situations confuse me," she muttered,
wondering how to explain her fears to a man who
exuded polished elegance with the same ease as he
breathed. "I tend to make a mess of things. I don't
want to embarrass you."

"If you're not used to these parties, I can see how
they might be intimidating."

She restrained her impulse to hug him. "I'm not
intimidated so much as terrified."

"Okay, I'll give you a few pointers. I'm an expert, so stick with me and you'll be fine. First, you look fabulous. Every woman will be wild with jealousy. Count any barbs as a compliment. Second, the men will be curious about your past—the less you tell them, the more desirable you'll become."

"What about conversation?"

He cast her a devastating smile. "If you get stuck, talk about the weather. Or the flight over. And I've found when I have no idea what someone is saying to me, it's useful to nod wisely and say, 'Really.'"

"Really?" She grinned.

He took her elbow and escorted her out of the hotel. "Works like a charm."

Despite his attempt to reassure her, by the time a valet parked their car at the party, a bevy of butterflies fluttered in her stomach. An experienced international traveler, he'd instructed her to keep her passport with her at all times, and during the car ride, he'd asked her to place his documents in her purse. But on such short notice, not even Ford's pull had enabled him to secure bodyguards until tomorrow.

The sounds of classical music with conversations in a dozen languages drifted outside a massive stone building with soaring columns. She'd hoped for a party of less than fifty people, but that many guests filled the well-worn entrance steps alone. She clutched the purse to her side, and Ford gripped her hand tightly.

"I don't feel too well," she told him, and it wasn't a lie. Her head throbbed and she couldn't blame it on the scent of heady perfumes combined with cigar smoke. Why had she allowed him to talk her into this? She should have stayed at the hotel where she belonged. She didn't belong here. She didn't belong with him.

"You'll be fine. Take a deep breath," he murmured.

She inhaled and let the air out slowly.

"Better?"

"This will end badly, I can feel it."

"It's your nerves talking. Security around the embassy is always tight. We're safe here."

"I'll do something to embarrass you, I know it."

Ford offered her his arm. "If embarrassing me is all that you're worried about, well, then, I forgive you."

She shook her head but couldn't restrain a nervous giggle. Unsure how he'd accomplished it, she realized he'd made her worries seem absurd. "But you don't know what I've done yet!"

"Exactly. So now you won't have to worry, since I've already forgiven you."

"This is the most ridiculous conversation I've ever had." She sighed in resignation as he whisked her through the entrance and into a crowd of elegant women in designer gowns chatting in several languages with debonair men in black tuxedos. But her gaze wasn't on the people surrounding them. It was on Ford. "Did anyone ever tell you you're impossible?"

Before he could answer, a shot sounded. Women screamed. Without hesitation, she flung herself at Ford, tackling him to the floor.

Chapter Four

What the hell?

Ford had known Denise was edgy, but at the popping sound, she'd exploded, lunged at his hips and mowed him down like an NFL linebacker. He slammed to his back amid a crowd of party-goers. As air burst from his lungs, the chandelier overhead turned into multicolored spinning stars.

Before he could draw a breath, Denise flattened herself on his chest, knocking any remaining wind out of him. When she cradled his head beneath her shoulder in a protective gesture, breathing became impossible.

He pushed on her shoulder, and she raised herself partially off him. Her topaz eyes looked into his and he counted four of them and two noses.

"Are you all right?" she asked.

With the air sucked out of his lungs, he couldn't speak. Face white, her gestures frantic, she patted his shoulders, his chest, his stomach, searching for an injury. "Are you hit?"

He grabbed her hands before she moved her inspection lower and he responded in a manner that would embarrass them both. Despite his tortured lungs, her silky skin pressed to him was already heating his blood. Hell! He shouldn't be reacting to her.

A crowd encircled them and several high-pitched laughs mixed with outright chuckles. His vision settled, refocusing her face.

Biting her lip, Denise paid no attention to the curious onlookers. Her wild-eyed gaze centered on him. "Talk to me, damn it!"

Her tawny eyes darkened with concern, and she couldn't have looked more gorgeous. Her gown tangled about him, and with her hair cascading around her shoulders and her makeup smudged, she'd never looked more desirable. He yearned to take her into his arms and kiss the frightened look off her face. That is, when he could breathe again.

"I'm fine," he finally gasped.

"You don't sound fine. You can't even breathe. Should I call an ambulance?"

His rib cage expanded and he filled his starving lungs amid a few hacking coughs. "There was nothing wrong with my breathing until you tackled me and pounced on my chest."

Her head jerked and she stiffened. "The shot—"

"The champagne cork popping out of the bottle didn't hit me."

For the first time, Denise spied the crowd milling around them. The music had stopped. As comprehension glimmered in her eyes and she realized she'd created a scene, a crimson blush rose from her breasts to her neck to her cheeks.

"Damn! I told you I don't do parties." Her shoulders trembled, and she lifted her knuckles to her mouth. "I didn't—"

"It's okay." He sat up slowly, biting back a groan. She'd obviously thought she was saving his life from a bullet. He'd never forget how courageously she'd shielded him with her body. A very interesting body. Beneath her curves, she had the well-conditioned muscle tone of a trained athlete. He could still feel the imprint of her breasts molding to his chest, her heart thumping as she'd protected him. But his hand cradling her bottom was the physical imprint that seized his imagination. She had the most delicious backside, round and firm and lush, and earlier he couldn't resist lagging behind her so he could enjoy the surefooted sway of her hips. A surge of desire curled in his stomach, but now was not the time for such thoughts.

Chest heaving, Denise scooped up her purse and scrambled to her feet. She lifted a glass of champagne from a passing waiter and polished it off like a longshoreman downing a boilermaker. Her eyes darted back and forth like a cornered animal's. Recalling her prior concerns about attending this party, he suspected she was about to flee, run off where she could be alone to lick her wounds.

He had to stop her from leaving, but at the moment, he was in no condition to chase her. Forcing himself to concentrate on inhaling and exhaling, he thought about regaining his feet.

He let out a small groan and held out his hand. "Could you help me up?"

"Show's over," she muttered. The music resumed and the crowd drifted away as she leaned down to take his hand. Surprising him with her strength, she pulled him up, her eyes a mixture of anger, worry and pure misery.

"You don't think I broke any ribs, do you?" she asked.

"I'd be more than glad to check yours after we return to the hotel," he teased, deliberately misunderstanding her.

She glared at him. "I'm not some overnight floozy."

Good. The anger he'd provoked would give her the internal fortitude to face the still-tittering crowd. When she started to move away, he let his knees buckle, putting more weight on her shoulders and pinning her to his side. The skin of her shoulder beneath his forearm was downy soft, and the flesh of her arm just as velvety, though toned with firm muscles. Her combination of softness and hardness appealed to him on a level he didn't wish to examine too carefully. He'd already made one mistake with Lindsay Betancourt. He had no wish to make another.

Cane tapping, Bruce Willowby stepped toward them, clearly ready to offer assistance, but with a nod, Ford declined his offer and gestured him away, asking Denise instead, "Can you help me outside for some fresh air?"

"Gladly." He bit back a comment about her relief to be heading out of the party.

She led him toward the front door, but before he took two steps, a silver-haired gentleman approached with a mincing gait but perfect posture, his gnarled hand outstretched and shaking with old age. "Gustave Druary."

Keeping one arm over Denise's shoulder to prevent her from slipping sway, Ford shook Gustave's arthritic hand. "And this is Denise Ward." As she offered her hand and Gustave raised it to his lips with a creaky bow, Ford told her, "Mr. Druary owns Swiss National Bank of Geneva."

The banker's horsey face broke into a careful smile. "Call me Gustave. I'm sorry to arrive late. I just came in and heard about the excitement. A woman mistook the pop of a champagne cork for a gunshot." He clucked his tongue against the roof of a mouth wrinkled with frown lines. "Now, that's a heroic woman, one that would risk her life for a man's."

Beneath his arm, Denise trembled, but she held her ground.

"We should all be so fortunate." Ford didn't wait for Gustave to respond, but continued, steering the topic in the direction he wanted. "And speaking of fortunes, I've been wondering if you might do me a small favor?"

Gustave handed him a business card, his shrewd old eyes probing and assessing. "I understand you are interested in buying a home in Monaco, *monsieur?*"

Denise's eyebrows knotted. Apparently, she hadn't yet caught on that Gustave was willing to sell them the information. In exchange for the details they wanted from the banker, Ford would pay a premium price for a home in Monaco. The bribe would appear a simple business transaction, and if Ford paid too much for the home, no one except his business partner, Martin, would question the purchase.

Ford lifted a flute of champagne from a passing waiter and handed it to Denise, then took another for himself. Their fingers touched and their eyes met, hers revealing a dawning comprehension. He clinked her glass with his before turning back to Gustave. "I'm quite fond of the principality. I vacation there every few years. A home in the area would be convenient."

Gustave's rheumy eyes didn't blink. "The favor, *monsieur?*"

Ford handed him a slip of paper with the transaction they wanted traced. "I'd like information on the recipient."

"What kind of information?"

"Anything you've got. A name, a description, an address, a forwarding bank account."

Gustave placed the paper in his coat pocket. "I'll see what I can do. Where can I reach you tomorrow?"

"I'll be in touch. It's been a pleasure." After the men shook hands, he and Denise continued through the swirling crowd toward the front door. Handing off her untouched drink to a waiter, she still wore a haunted look in her eyes.

No longer the center of attention, she'd stopped trembling, and her face, although alive with color, had lost its crimson blush. "You're paying too much for the house in Monaco in exchange for the information. Is that legal?"

"Is it justice to allow Rhonda's murderer to go free?" he countered. "I'm just buying a house."

"One you haven't seen."

"I buy things I haven't seen almost every day."

"That doesn't make it prudent."

Amused at her indignation, he restrained himself to cocking one eyebrow. Besides if he laughed, his ribs would hurt and pride demanded he maintain a don't-give-a-damn, uninjured air. "Are you sure you're the same woman who kidnapped me?" he countered.

The music faded as they ambled outside. As they descended broad steps between imposing columns that led to the street, Denise shivered from the brisk night air. He wrapped his arm around her waist, drawing her tighter to him.

She let out a small sound at the closeness, then stiffened and tried to pull away. "I don't normally take on kidnapping assignments. You were the exception."

He kept her there a second longer, then reluctantly released her. "Of course. I'm an exceptional man and you can't resist me."

"I wouldn't go that far," she retorted. "Although you do have your moments."

They walked down the rest of the steps, and he thought about taking her back into his arms and kissing her. Perhaps letting his fingers wander from her shoulders to the small of her back and lower to her lush—

"Get down!" Denise called out, tugging his wrist, jerking him forward.

Ford swore. *Not again.* His ribs weren't up to another pounding.

Seemingly out of nowhere, a spray of chalk rained onto his face. He glanced at one of the columns to see a bullet lodged in a crater behind the spot where his head had just been. Adrenaline surged through him. Although he hadn't heard a shot, someone had just tried to kill him!

She'd saved his life.

How had she known?

While he tried to figure out what had happened, Denise yanked him around the column. They merged with a group of chattering Spaniards who remained oblivious to the shooting.

She kept her throaty voice low, urgent. "We need to find another way out. Fast. The sniper has a silencer. He went for a head shot. Probably a pro."

The same modus operandi as the one used by the Black Rose.

He had no idea how she moved so quickly on those high heels, but as the sounds of conversation engulfed them, they reached the building under the protective cover of the unknowing Spanish diplomats. Holding her hand tightly, he tugged her through the crowd. Worried that once they reached the street she'd be a prime target in her spectacular gold-sequined gown, he searched for words to convince her to leave him.

After shouldering past a dancing couple, he spoke urgently, "The assassin's after me. Let's split up. I'll meet you back at the hotel."

Her voice was urgent but lacking panic. "We can't return to the hotel. We can't take your car. And if you want to live, you can't leave me behind. We have to sneak out of here."

She was right. Lord knew, she was better at the complexities and difficulties of cloak-and-dagger work than he was. He could solve their problems with his cell phone, but it remained at the hotel with their luggage. Still, phone or no phone, he wouldn't put her life at risk, and he could only think of one way to make her stay behind.

He guided her toward the kitchen. "In that gold

gown, you'll stand out like a Krugerrand in a pile of nickels."

"You're right." She stayed with him as they threaded their way past white-coated chefs in tall white hats rushing to and fro between stoves, ovens and countertops, dinnerware and pots clinking and clanging. Amid the chaos, the fragrance of garlic, butter, onions, chicken and cream sauces made his mouth water, his stomach rumble, but he kept looking over his shoulder for the assassin. Feeding his empty belly was the least of his worries.

Relief flooded him that she'd agreed to split up. Before he could name a place to meet later, she dug in her heels and hauled him to a screeching stop.

He twisted around, expecting to be shot at. When nothing happened, he turned to her with a frown. "What?"

"I need clothes and a translator." She dragged him over to a woman wearing jeans and a sweater.

He'd misunderstood, he realized. She hadn't agreed to leave him but had simply acknowledged her dress made her a target. And she'd left him to make the awkward explanation in French.

Sixty seconds later, the two women stripped to their underwear in the middle of the kitchen while he stood protectively nearby, searching for a killer. The chefs, cooks and their helpers bustled around the trio as if they didn't exist. No one except Ford seemed to notice anything unusual. The chefs kept their eyes on their work. The waiters entered with empty trays and left with refills. Perhaps they all thought the women were part of some acting troupe—entertainment for the guests.

Although he kept a sharp watch for danger, he wasn't immune to Denise in her strapless bra and gold-colored panties. Turning his back to avoid staring, he searched for the killer, but he couldn't banish Denise's lovely figure from his mind. Her lean muscles and firm curves proved an almost irresistible distraction.

Hurriedly dumping the contents from her purse to the woman's handbag, Denise used precious seconds to zip their passports into a side pocket. After she'd dressed, he found breathing easier. The huge navy sweater was loose, and the tight jeans clung to her hips like leggings, but with all her gorgeous skin once again covered, he'd regained his composure.

She smoothed down her sweater and joined him. "The shoes fit. Come on, let's go."

He looked left, right, back over his shoulder. "We should split up."

"No way. I don't speak French. I'd get lost. The Black Rose could find me."

"He's not after you." No matter how much he'd miss her company, he wouldn't risk her life. A woman with Denise's street smarts would be better off alone in a strange country than burdened by him with the Black Rose on his tail.

Searching for a side exit, he removed his bowtie and his dark jacket and rolled up the white sleeves of his shirt to appear more casual. She led him behind a pastry shelf to a door. A bread truck had backed into the narrow alley, blocking their exit. He was about to turn around and look for another way out when she climbed into the truck.

She slid a basket of bread rolls aside and merged

into the shadows. "We can discuss it later. Right now, let's get out of the building. We need to put as much distance between the embassy and us as we can, as quickly as we can."

DAMN THE BRADDACK LUCK! The man had more lives than the proverbial cat, and the woman P.I. with him was an additional complication. Why couldn't Braddack follow his usual pattern of dating society debutantes? Ford must have hired Denise Ward. Nothing else could explain their showing up at Grendal's farmhouse. Somehow the woman had found a clue to Rhonda's death, and Ford was now following though on his vow to find Rhonda's killer.

Too bad he wouldn't succeed. Too much time had passed. All tracks had been covered.

Still, it paid to be careful. With all the trouble Braddack caused, he deserved to die slowly. But there was no more time for games.

Their escape at the embassy was only a minor setback. They were on foot, in a foreign country. No doubt Braddack couldn't go an hour without using a credit card. And the P.I. was out of her league, no longer up against cheating husbands and deadbeat dads, but the Black Rose, the most renowned assassin in Europe.

They wouldn't last the night.

FORD LEAPED INTO the truck after Denise, the scent of fresh-baked bread welcoming him and reminding him of his growing hunger. As he followed her past long French breads and braided loaves of wheat and rye, he replaced the baskets she'd moved. Toward the front, she'd cleared a space between two rows of shelving where they leaned against the truck's inner wall.

Helping herself to a flaky croissant, she munched while giving him another. He sat beside her, wincing at his sore ribs, and accepted her offering. "When we left the party, how did you know about—"

"The sniper?"

"Yes."

Wedged into the cramped space, she was forced to lean against him. He put his arm around her, liking the way her shoulders fit. A tendril of long curly hair drifted across his cheek and it was hard to remember such a feminine bundle could think so fast on her feet. She'd saved his life tonight, and words of thanks seemed inadequate. His admiration for her soared at her unusual display of courage. While she hadn't hesitated to tackle him earlier, now she tried to edge away so they didn't touch, letting him know she was more affected by him than she'd admit.

Dim streetlights filtered through the open metal door of the bread truck and reflected on her face. Her eyes revealed the strain. Were her instincts telling her he wanted to do more than sit by her side? If she knew what he was thinking, she'd probably punch him in the nose.

"Don't tell me your instincts warned you about the sniper?"

She swallowed the last of her croissant and plucked another from the shelf beside them. As she spoke, a crumb at the corner of her mouth tantalized him. "It was luck. A car's headlights glinted off the gun barrel."

He bit into his own dinner. The treat melted in his mouth. "That wasn't luck. You were alert and ready to act. I didn't see him." And he should have.

"No doubt you had other things on your mind," she said dryly.

He thought back to the moment just before the shot and recalled he'd been considering whether to kiss her. From the sound of her tone just now, he wondered if she'd surmised his intention. Such distractions could get them killed.

From now on, he'd stick to the business at hand. Besides, while he no longer doubted his attraction to her, Denise clearly detested his life-style. He couldn't imagine her attending parties or golf tournaments, a mere ornament on his arm.

Like Rhonda had been?

That wasn't a fair question. His former wife had enjoyed the parties, enjoyed the social whirl that aided his career. She'd often teased him that he'd accomplished more on the golf course than in the office.

As he lifted a rye loaf, bit into the still-warm crust and chewed, the flavor of caraway seeds burst in his mouth. He mulled over his past. Rhonda had seemed content to run her life around his in a way Denise never would. It had been convenient.

But he didn't need convenience—not when his soul cried out for something more. Yet, he had to regain control of his thoughts. He'd already made a mistake by thinking Lindsay Betancourt was the right woman for him. He barely thought of her at all, and when he did, it was with relief not regret. On the other hand, when he closed his eyes, Denise's image burned his mind. But her features were only part of the attractive package. She had intelligence and courage and had just saved his life.

Outside, footsteps approached, interrupting his thoughts. The metal door swung shut with a clang, blocking out the streetlights that had flickered inside. Denise's every muscle stiffened to an unnatural tautness.

Ford stood and looked through the tiny window into the cab. The man wore a uniform. "Relax. It's the regular driver."

He scooted back beside her. She remained stiff as three-day-old bread.

"What's wrong?" he whispered.

"Nothing."

"You're shaking."

"It's just the truck's vibration." She wasn't a good liar. Her voice caught and fluttered.

The truck pulled around a corner, but the occasional pothole couldn't account for her trembling. Perhaps the shocks she'd suffered were catching up with her. They'd traveled almost nonstop to discover a dead body. He'd forced her to attend a party. Then an assassin had shot at them. During the action, she'd held tough, in control. Now they were stuck in the back of a bread truck on their way to who-knew-where—but they were still relatively safe. So why was she shaking? What had suddenly made her so vulnerable?

And why was his conscience screaming at him to protect her? But from what?

She gripped his hand so tightly she cut off the circulation. "I don't like the dark."

He pulled a lighter out of his pocket and flicked it

on. The small flame reflected the panic in her eyes. After a moment in the light, her dilated pupils returned to usual size. Her breathing evened out and she spoke almost normally. "You don't smoke, do you?"

Now he was the one uncomfortable. He didn't want to admit that when he could no longer stand the loneliness, he used the lighter to strike up conversations with women. "Should we get off the truck at the next stop?"

"It depends." Her voice cracked.

"On what?"

"Whether or not we stop in the city. Let's hope the assassin didn't have a partner watching the back door and that we're not being tailed." She drew her knees to her chest and wrapped her arms around them but he could still feel her trembling.

"No one watching could know for certain that we're in this truck." He ached to reassure her, but she was shutting him out, and he didn't like it one bit.

"But if the assassin traipses into the party and learns we're not there, he'll guess we escaped. He may assume we left on foot or hailed a cab. But if he thinks to ask, it won't take long to discover which trucks left and by which route."

His stomach did a jig. He'd taken for granted they were safe. That kind of assumption could get them killed. The Black Rose had had more than an entire year to learn about Ford's contacts, his mode of travel, his friends. They would have to avoid Ford's usual haunts.

"You have our passports, don't you?" he asked.

"Why?"

He steadied them as the truck rounded a corner. "We need to get you on the first flight home."

Her shaking worsened. "*We* can't fly from Switzerland. We'll have to cross the border."

"But customs—"

"We're not going through customs."

He almost choked on the last bit of rye. "Hold it right there. Tomorrow morning, we'll have professional bodyguards to protect us. We can—"

"We need to disappear, not pick up an entourage," she whispered insistently. "If the Black Rose is as good as Willowby said, he'll have the airports, bus and train stations covered. We can't even rent a car."

"One person couldn't possibly cover that much territory."

"Once you use a credit card, your name pops into a computer database. Presto, you've been traced." She turned to him, and brushed her hair from her face. "How much cash have you got on you?"

"A few thousand. Why?"

"I don't know yet. I'm taking stock of our assets. Once Gustave gives us information on those bank accounts, we can decide our next move. Meanwhile, tomorrow, I want to research black roses. Maybe we'll get lucky and they'll be rare."

"I don't follow."

"If every flower shop in Europe sells black roses, tracing the flowers down will be impossible. But if they are expensive, there will be fewer sales, fewer buyers to track. Sales records of black roses might lead us to the assassin."

"If we need more cash, just give me ten minutes in a bank—"

"I don't want to risk it unless we have to. Any computer transaction with your name attached might be traced."

His lighter winked out. Despite his attempts to re-light it, the sparks wouldn't catch. "Sorry, out of fuel."

"Tell me the walls aren't closing in." She tried to joke, but she couldn't disguise the tremble in her voice.

Her mixture of bravado and fear had confused him. But now that he understood she didn't like being con-fined inside the dark bread truck, he tried to reassure her. "Hey, it'll be okay."

Panic edged her words. "We might be stuck in here all night."

He rubbed his hand back and forth over her arm, trying to heat her icy skin. "No chance of that. He has too much inventory to deliver."

"You think so?"

He searched for a way to take her mind off the darkness. "Close your eyes."

"Why?" Her voice cracked.

"Pretend you're someplace safe. In bed."

"I never think of being in bed with you as safe." Her muscles went rigid at her admission. She must be terrified of the dark to confess to thinking about him, and he refused to take advantage of her vulnerability and pursue the intriguing topic.

Just the thought of what she'd suggested caused his forehead to bead with sweat. Was it so obvious that he wanted to kiss her? Or hold her? She was right. Sharing a bed with him would be anything but safe.

"Come on," he coaxed. "Close your eyes. Mine are shut. Rest your head on my shoulder. I won't bite."

"You've probably bitten so many women, you can do it with your eyes closed," she muttered.

From the way she pressed against him, so hard his ribs ached, he knew the sarcasm was to keep her fear at bay. Her breathing came in ragged gulps. Every muscle tightened into hard knots.

The contradictions in her amazed him. She was afraid of the dark and terrified of social blunders, yet fearless of assassins, protecting him with her own body from an imagined bullet. The thought gave him a warm feeling.

She'd jumped into the bread truck without hesitation, knowing she was petrified of the dark. Shy about wearing a revealing ball gown, she hadn't hesitated to change her clothes in the middle of a kitchen filled with men. She ran like the wind, yet had the silkiest, softest skin.

As he held her, he tried to forget her comment about the two of them in bed. But breathing in her vanilla scent, it was impossible not to imagine making love to her. What would she be like? Tender kitten or passionate tigress?

The truck's brakes squealed. Another red light? Or had they reached a stop along the bread route?

As they rolled to a halt, she jumped to her feet, lunged toward the back of the truck. He grabbed her, pulling her back to his chest. Her heart beat frantically against him. Smoothing the hair from her clammy forehead, he sensed that only her strong will kept her from screaming and pounding his shoulders to be free. "Hey, just another minute," he told her. "Let him open the door and make his delivery. Then we'll sneak out."

The door banged open with a clang. Their driver picked up two baskets and wandered away whistling.

"Let's go."

She leaped away from him like a cat on fire. Dashing toward the truck's exit, she tripped over a basket. Bread rolled to the floor but it didn't slow her. He followed as quickly as he could.

The truck had stopped in another alley. The damp pavement smelled of oil and tar. Garbage overflowed a receptacle, the stench of rotten food lay heavy in the murky air. A cobbled street led between rows of houses with belching chimneys that spread a pall over the night sky.

Hand in hand, they trekked past stone buildings toward the streetlights. Ford checked his watch. "It's one-thirty. We were in the truck about half an hour."

"It seemed like forever." Her voice sounded close to normal now.

"We must still be in the city. On the outskirts, I'd guess."

The medieval architecture and colorful fountains that dominated the central part of the city near the embassy had changed to picturesque cobblestone streets lined with flower-decked houses and shops. The road held few cars. A dog barked at the full moon which was partially blocked by puffy clouds. The streets were relatively deserted.

"Let's put as much distance between us and the

bread truck as possible,'' Denise suggested, picking up their pace with newfound confidence.

Now that she'd escaped the confining darkness of the truck, she'd lost her nervousness. They might be lost in a foreign city, but that didn't frighten her. His urge to get them off the streets before they ran into trouble warred with the need to leave town.

Traveling by train or plane or rental car was out of the question. Buses didn't run at this time of night.

"Why don't I call a taxi?" he suggested.

"I'd rather not. The assassin could trace the bread truck's route, call the taxi companies and ask if anyone was picked up near where the truck stopped. From there, it would be simply a matter of talking to the driver to find us."

"You're good at this."

"Think again. Evading a professional assassin is a lot more difficult than tracking a father avoiding child support. My on-the-job competency is the equivalent of making the mail clerk CEO of Norton Industries."

He squeezed her hand. "I would be dead if it weren't for you."

She fluffed off his praise. "And we may not last a day on the streets if we don't do some quick maneuvering."

The streets remained empty except for a couple just leaving their apartment. Denise pointed at two bicycles locked against a wrought-iron railing. "Ford, try and buy their bikes."

He approached the pair and spoke softly in French in order not to frighten the hesitant couple. Money could be a powerful inducement to sell, especially when he offered double the price of new bikes. With their finances several thousand francs poorer, they climbed onto the bikes.

"What did you say to them?" Denise shifted gears, her long golden hair flying behind her.

"I told them we were on our honeymoon and our bikes were stolen."

She looked over at him skeptically. "That's it?"

"I mentioned we had a hotel reservation and if we didn't arrive soon, our first night together wouldn't happen."

She let out a low whistle. "You are some liar."

He wished he hadn't been lying. For a moment he wished they *were* on their honeymoon, on the way to their hotel—not fleeing the country, attempting to cross the border pursued by an assassin who might even now be tracking them.

"Where to?" he asked.

"We should head for the border. That way we can keep our options open depending on what Gustave finds out for us."

They rode the bikes, heading west, then north, then west again toward France, taking short breaks when needed. If he remembered his geography correctly, they weren't far from the Swiss-French border. Unfortunately, the Jura Mountains separated the two countries. Although less rugged than the Alps, three- to five-thousand-foot ridges created a notable barrier to crossing the border. Once they reached Lake Neuchâtel, they'd be forced to head north to Basel or southwest to Geneva where the Black Rose could spot them at a checkpoint.

He drew beside her to converse. "Do you think the assassin works alone?"

"Why?"

Ford made his voice reasonable. "He can't cover every road out of Switzerland."

"True. But he'll have contacts, spies, people who feed him information. Right now, he probably has no idea where we are." She spoke urgently. "I see no reason to leave Switzerland. We're close to identifying him."

Had he missed something? "And how do you know we're close to identifying him?"

"Because he's out to kill us."

He groaned at her logic.

From behind them, a car's headlights caught them in its glare. He pulled farther off the road. Exposed and vulnerable on their bikes, he drew closer to Denise. She'd just said they were probably safe. She'd also told him she wasn't qualified for this job. His heart pounded as the light caught them in its glare once more.

Were they in trouble? Had the assassin found them?

"Don't look back," she warned.

"The vehicle is slowing." He glanced to his side and his stomach clenched as he gauged the distance to the trees and possible safety. Too far. "We'll never make it into the forest. Any suggestions?"

"Pray."

Chapter Five

Even a ten-year-old with a squirt gun couldn't miss a shot at Denise and Ford silhouetted by the nearing vehicle's headlights. Clutching the gun in her purse, she didn't withdraw the weapon, her heart racing like an Olympic biker crossing the finish line.

The car pulled parallel with them and stopped, and a man called out in German, *"Guten Abend."*

"Bonsoir." Hello, Ford replied in French.

The stranger's response sounded French. She glanced at Ford. "What does he want?"

"I'm not sure."

She climbed off her bike and edged closer to Ford. "If he was the Black Rose, we'd already be dead."

Ford exhaled softly. "Is that supposed to be comforting?"

The man exited his vehicle, leaving his engine running and his lights on. Of medium height and with a paunch draping his belt, he lumbered toward them. Although he carried himself with authority, he wasn't wearing a uniform.

As the men conversed, she peered into his car, spotting a police radio next to a half-eaten sandwich.

He might be an off-duty officer, but why had he stopped them?

The assassin probably knew the people and geography of this country a hell of a lot better than she did. And while biking tourists were more common during summer, many Americans vacationed in Europe during the early fall. Could he have tapped into the police computer system and uploaded false data about them? Or was her revved-up imagination verging on paranoia?

At Ford's responses, the German scratched his head and eyed her as if she were crazy. Wishing she'd studied French, she shifted uneasily in the grass. Ford squeezed her hand, as if to say he had the conversation under control, and she appreciated his gesture.

With a nod, the other man finally returned to his car and drove off. She released her pent-up breath. "Well?"

"He said Neuchâtel is about ten kilometers up the road."

They climbed back on their bikes, and headed west. She drew beside him to converse. "That's all? Why did he stop?"

Ford eased his pedaling and rubbed his jaw as if perplexed. "He said night was an odd time for tourists to be bike riding. And, he looked at my tuxedo pants and dress shirt strangely. Can't say I blame him. He asked where we're headed."

Alarm washed over her. "You told him?"

"I thought having a destination would look better than running away."

"Sorry, you're right. Not understanding the language makes me tense." She supposed the stranger was harmless. Ford hadn't spoken their names and they hadn't shown identification. But the man could describe them and their destination. The edginess at the back of her stomach wouldn't go away.

"How'd you grow up in Louisiana without learning at least some Cajun French?" Ford picked up the pace.

"I thought business courses would be more useful." Rhonda had studied French, Spanish and German with no thought of a career, while Denise had wanted her own business. They had never competed with one another, not over school or men. Denise hadn't coveted any man Rhonda had dated. Until Ford. And she wouldn't take advantage of Rhonda's death by pursuing Ford now—no matter how many sparks sizzled between them. "A lot of good economics and business courses are doing me now."

"All knowledge comes in handy. My brother, Max, is an inventor. In a pinch he can make perfume or a bomb. He's earned a fortune from his inventions but you'd never know it by the way he lives."

"You don't approve?" Her legs ached, and talking helped keep her mind off muscles throbbing from unaccustomed use. At home, she jogged daily, but biking used different muscles. Her rear might never recover.

"Living on a plantation suits Max. He works in the lab out back and leaves the farming to employees so he can spend time with his family. For fun he races speedboats on the world circuit."

"What do your parents think?"

"They approve of Max and me. Although they

don't understand why I'm so driven in business, they'll back me as long as I'm happy.''

''What do your parents do?'' she asked.

''Mother spends a lot of time hosting charity events. Red enjoys his retirement and keeps busy playing golf. Both do their own thing while trying to keep up with their granddaughter, Skye.''

His parents sounded ideal. Her parents had shown their love through the strictness of discipline, afraid if they coddled her too much, she would grow up spoiled. How would she have turned out if her parents had given her more freedom? ''Your family sounds wonderful.''

''They are. I love them.'' His simple words echoed in the night air.

Soon the road narrowed, dark pines closed around them and the sweet scent of resin mingled with wildflowers and grasses. The road edged a gurgling brook for a while in the moonlight, and she'd have thought their journey romantic if she weren't so tired, thirsty and worried about the Black Rose's pursuit.

As if risking their lives wasn't enough, she was finding it harder and harder to control her infatuation with Ford. She couldn't forget his strong arms gently cradling her in the truck. Smelling enticingly of cedar, he'd felt so good, she'd ached to burrow under his shirt and run her palms over his skin.

Shifting on the hard seat, she tried to ignore his physical closeness. ''You and Max were identical twins, yet your parents encouraged you to follow your own interests. Mine wanted me to be like Rhonda, head cheerleader, homecoming queen, Miss Popularity.'' He turned his head sharply, and she wished she could see his eyes. "There's nothing wrong with what Rhonda chose, it just wasn't the life I wanted. My goals are different from my parents' hopes for me, so no matter what I accomplish, I'll always be a failure in their eyes."

His resonant voice wrapped around her like a warm blanket. "That's not fair to you."

No kidding. She spoke past the tightness in her throat. "In some ways, my parents' attitude has made me tough. I know how to choose what I want, how to say no. I'm not afraid to try new things. And I've failed often enough to know it won't kill me."

He remained silent for several minutes, then spoke so softly she almost didn't hear him above the noise of the wheels. "Rhonda thought she was a failure when she miscarried."

"She thought if she couldn't give you a child, she'd lose your love." Denise coasted to give her legs a rest.

"I told her she was all the family I needed, but she insisted on going to a fertility clinic. That's when Norton Industries bought the Kine clinic and I became a member of the board of directors. Rhonda never complained about the painful fertility shots. When the test-tube baby was finally implanted, she was so happy I thought maybe the pain and heartache had been worth it. When the miscarriage almost killed her, I forbid her to try again. I didn't want her risking her health. I didn't want to lose her." He shook his head. "I'm not sure what I could have done differently."

She guessed he'd agonized for a long time over the past, but hadn't imagined him so torn by guilt. "You mustn't blame yourself. Children were vital to Rhonda.''

''Sometimes I think she wanted them more to please me than for herself.''

His insight surprised her. Had her cousin wanted to be a cheerleader and homecoming queen, or had she pursued those goals to please parents, teachers and friends? Perhaps she hadn't known Rhonda as well as she'd thought.

''I failed to convince her she was enough to keep me happy.'' His words turned harsh, bitter. ''I blame myself for her death.''

''Why?'' Despite the warmth generated by the long bike ride, a shiver rippled down Denise's spine. She studied his granite expression, but shadows hid the distress she knew he must be feeling.

''The day she died, we'd taken a helicopter up the mountain to ski on the glaciers. We'd been on the slope only ten minutes, and I'd skied a bit ahead. When another chopper flew overhead, I paid little attention, thinking it carried more skiers. And then—'' He stopped speaking.

Rhonda had died months ago, but time hadn't lessened his mourning. The endless, dark road in the cold empty countryside and her physical discomfort magnified her grief. ''Tell me the rest.''

''I pulled up to wait for Rhonda and saw several puffs of snow burst above her. Gunshots from the helicopter started the avalanche.''

Denise sighed, wishing she didn't need to hear the rest of the story. But there were gaps in the police reports and stories in the press. Any new information might help them identify the assassin. ''I couldn't trace a name from the helicopter's rental agreement. The assassin paid cash for the flight. The pilot disappeared. He must have used a fake name because my contacts couldn't find anything on him.''

"If I hadn't survived, everyone would have assumed the avalanche was a freak accident.''

His countenance didn't change, but his voice lowered. Only her growing sensitivity allowed her to recognize the agony he was feeling.

"A recent warming trend had loosened the snow,'' he continued. "After the gunshots, the mountain shook. Rhonda fell and tumbled. A wall of snow broke off the mountain's face and slid, the roar of falling snow louder than thunder. She screamed my name. I tried to reach her, but snow swept me away, and I landed in a protected pocket. But she was buried beneath twenty feet of snow.''

Tears burned her eyes and she brushed them away with the back of her hand.

"It wasn't your fault.''

"If I'd stayed next to her, I might have saved her.''

"You'd have died together,'' she insisted. "You're feeling guilt because you survived and she didn't.''

His voice turned icy cold. "How do you know what I feel?''

"I loved her, too.'' He remained silent, and she coasted to a stop. "Are you okay?''

He halted, too. "I've been better.''

She wished for the right words to comfort him. "The grief never goes away completely, at least for me it hasn't. I don't care what psychologists say, getting even, revenge, justice—whatever you call it— will repay my debt and help ease the grief.''

"I loved her." His words slipped out slowly, as if against his will. "She was the perfect wife. I should have known better than to propose to Lindsay Betancourt. No one could replace Rhonda."

A subdued shudder rippled through her. He'd spoken with such matter-of-fact calm, but she heard the truth in his words. Rhonda had been sweet, loving, kind. Perfect. Any disloyal thoughts she'd had of taking her cousin's place in Ford's heart died.

"I miss her, still," he said. "Scotch didn't help. Neither did working longer hours. Or other women. By marrying Lindsay, I hoped to regain what I'd lost, but the part of me that wanted to be a husband died with Rhonda. How could I have been so stupid?"

"You were hurting and vulnerable." She identified with his sorrow, the gut-wrenching burning inside at the thought of Rhonda's needless death. If she could never repay Rhonda the debt she owed, at least she could find her killer.

"I don't know anything about marriage," she said, "but I suspect each couple is different. You can't expect another woman to be Rhonda. And if she tried, for your sake, she'd be someone she isn't."

Moonlight glinted on his grim lips as he started to pedal again. "Even if I did that with Lindsay, you still didn't have the right to kidnap me."

She rode slowly to keep pace. "Are you sorry you came?"

"I'm tired, sweaty and thirsty. This seat is getting harder by the second. Ask me later."

Leaving the pine forest behind, they found dawn brightening the sky. Sunlight broke through the mist-wrapped, blue-velveted mountains ahead, ending the intimacy they'd shared in the darkness.

She pointed toward church spires, tall towers, vine-yards and a sparkling lake. "That must be Neuchâtel. We're almost there."

Less than a half hour later, they proceeded through an ancient gate onto a wide avenue bustling with honking cars, the clop of horses' hooves and Swiss businessmen rustling their morning papers. Walking their bikes under dappled arches, they passed sand-stone buildings. Queen Anne's lace, lavender bells and pink alpenrose spilled out of flower boxes, their scent sweetening the morning air.

They agreed on an open café and crossed a charm-ing square dotted with tiny blue forget-me-nots, and purple pansies no bigger than a two-franc coin. After parking the bikes outside, they entered the café, greeted by the aroma of fresh-brewed coffee. At the enticing scent, Denise's mouth watered in anticipa-tion. "I'm starved. Order for me, please." She headed to the rest room.

On the way out, she gasped at the sight of herself in a mirror. Dirt streaked from her temple to her chin. Her hair was windblown and tangled. She grimaced. After washing her hands and face, she tamed her hair into a French braid.

She returned to their table to find Ford gone. Where was he? Her appetite diminished in a wave of con-cern. He'd left without an explanation.

She was just about to search for him, when he strolled through the café's front door as if he owned the place. His dark hair was slick, his black lashes spiked with water droplets. A dark shadow of a beard showed off his arrogant chin and the hard sculpted planes of his cheeks. He looked more handsome than he had a right to after spending the night on a bike. He'd obviously taken time to wash. But the men's room wasn't outside.

"Where did you go?"

Ford floated a napkin onto his lap. "I made some phone calls."

"Gustave was at the bank this early?"

"He has a reputation for being at his desk before dawn."

She leaned forward, anxious to hear. Gustave's information was critical in their search for the Black Rose. Following the banking trail and searching for sellers of black roses were the only clues they had. "So, what did he find out for us?"

Ford spread his hands, palms up. "Not as much as I'd like."

Her hopes plummeted. Had they come all this way to go home in defeat?

"Gustave was abrupt and sounded terrified," Ford continued. "He said the money entered the bank, and both times was transferred to London the same day. He claimed he didn't know the name on the account."

Denise drummed her fingers on the table. Those funds had been wired from Dr. Henschel's account in the United States to Bern, where Rhonda had been murdered, in two payments—one a week before her death, the second a day after. Following the money trail had not only become crucial to finding Rhonda's killer, but vital for them to stay alive. "Perhaps someone else at the bank—"

Ford shook his head. "No one else has access to what we need."

The Black Rose had closed down every lead. Grendal was dead. The banker wouldn't talk. They were at an impasse. The chance of finding Rhonda's killer seemed more remote than ever. Ford appeared to take the bad news in stride, yet, by the telltale muscle flickering in his jaw, she knew better. He wanted the assassin as badly as she did.

"I don't want to raise your hopes," he said, "but I phoned my partner. Martin and I discussed ways to trace the bank wire in England."

She frowned, not at all pleased he'd called the States. His partner might be his best friend, but that didn't mean Martin couldn't accidentally let their whereabouts slip to the wrong person. Norton Industries' phones could be tapped.

"What do you mean, you discussed ways to trace the transaction?"

"Norton Industries has friends in the British government with access to the information we need. In addition, I spoke to my secretary, Anne Baines—"

"That wasn't smart."

"It saved time. Sometimes risks have to be taken. Anne is a crackerjack researcher and has the resources to follow up on your suggestion about sellers of black roses. I asked her to look into where we could purchase black roses. We're on the run so it's a little difficult for anyone to call us back."

"You've just widened the circle of people who know where we are. If one of them slips, the Black Rose could pick up our trail again."

Ford ignored her scolding. "I trust my partner, and

I trust Anne. You brought me along to help. You wanted me to use my contacts. That's what I'm doing.''

She was probably being paranoid, but when he'd told her he'd made a call, her neck had started itching. Perhaps the sensation was just caused by dried sweat on her neck from the long bike ride. She settled for scratching, but she wanted a bath and she needed sleep. Complaining wouldn't erase the calls he'd made. If he'd somehow alerted the Black Rose to their whereabouts, she couldn't do much about it now.

But their partnership wouldn't work if he made decisions without consulting her. "Look, I'm sorry I snapped at you. But next time, before you call anyone, could we discuss it first?"

"Sure," he replied easily enough, but she could tell he thought she was overreacting.

Maybe she was. Her eyelids felt so heavy she could barely keep them open. She couldn't recall the last time she'd had a full night's sleep. "You think we could find a hotel room?"

"Come on." Ford stood, tossing bills onto the table. "We'll order room service at the hotel."

He found them a second-story room with adjoining doors that opened to a wraparound balcony overlooking the street. After breakfast, Denise showered and crawled into a plump bed, falling asleep almost as soon as her head hit the pillow.

SHATTERING GLASS awakened her, sending her thoughts whirling and her body rolling. Shards burst into the room, splattered across the floor, landing on the sheets and carpet.

A man plunged through her window. Her heart shot into her throat. She rolled to the far side of the bed, onto the floor, and grabbed the gun from her purse.

The man didn't move. For another second, she remained still. Who was he? Where had he come from?

She peered around the bed to see the stranger's eyes staring sightlessly at the ceiling. In the middle of his forehead was a bullet hole, in exactly the same place as Grendal's. Poor man. He never knew what hit him. One moment he was strolling along the balcony; the next, he was dead. Adrenaline surged through her, pushing away her urge to be sick.

Damn it! The Black Rose had found them.

Move. Self-preservation shifted her feet into high gear.

Grabbing her clothes, shoes and purse, she crawled to the unlocked door connecting to Ford's room. The assassin must have used a silencer since she'd never heard a shot. Apparently the breaking glass hadn't been loud enough to waken him. She dressed while she whispered to him. "Ford, wake up."

He didn't move until she leaned over to shake him.

Half-asleep, he reached around her waist and tugged, tumbling her into the bed with surprising force. She landed on his chest, his arms around her back, his hands on her bottom. His mouth captured hers, tasting of coffee and strawberry jam. His lips nibbled, teased and for one instant, she thrilled to the heat of his mouth, the insistence of his tongue, the strapping strength of his arms. He dug his fingers into her hair, his tongue stole into her mouth, taking her sweetly, passionately, roughly.

At any other time she might have melted into his

warmth, but she jerked back with a breathless gasp. "Hey!"

Cracking the window, a bullet whizzed by her ear, the whine inches from her face before it plunged into the opposite wall. As his window splintered, Ford's eyes opened sleepily, then sharpened and he released her.

She reached for his clothes, tossed them at him and kept rolling toward the window. "The Black Rose is out there. He just drilled a man between the eyes outside my room. We've got to leave. Now."

"I'm with you." Ford tugged on his crumpled slacks and slipped into his shoes. Shirt and jacket in hand, he simultaneously crouched and lunged toward the door. From the floor, he reached for the knob. A second bullet smashed into the door.

"Get down," she ordered. "The sniper has us pinned."

"Come with me," Ford insisted. "Since we don't know where he is, firing back can't cover our escape."

"I'll close the curtains." She accomplished the task from the floor, wincing as elbows and knees picked up a few slivers of glass. Ford tensed, ready to leap toward the door and into the hall.

"No! Not yet."

Ford hesitated.

The assassin squeezed off another round that hit inches from his last shot.

"Now. Go now!"

Ford yanked open the door and dived through the opening. A moment later she followed. He picked her up and set her on her feet. They sprinted toward the stairs that led to the street.

At the last minute, Ford held her back. "Won't he have the exits covered?"

"Maybe. Maybe not. He was shooting a rifle, using a silencer—that's why we never heard the shots. Let's hope he's too far away to cover all the exits."

Footsteps pounded toward them. Hotel security? Or had the assassin hired help? Whipping her head from side to side, she searched for cover. They were trapped in the hallway. She knocked on the nearest hotel-room door, found it already partway open and pushed inside with Ford on her heels.

A maid was vacuuming. Denise waved and the woman nodded and continued with her work, no doubt believing the room belonged to them.

Denise looked around thinking furiously. She spied a phone sitting atop a travel guide on the nightstand and formed a plan. "Call a cab to meet us at the back of the hotel."

Ford phoned while Denise peeked through the drapes. They hadn't much time. They were lucky the maid hadn't heard breaking glass over the vacuum. Someone would investigate the clamor soon though, find the body in her room and summon the police. They couldn't stay to answer questions, not with the assassin taking potshots at them.

Ford replaced the receiver. "No taxis. Buses, trains and canal boats are the local transportation. So I hired a horse and buggy."

The maid, who had been cleaning the shower, strode out of the bathroom, nodded a goodbye, then left. Denise waited until the door shut behind her.

"How long before the buggy arrives? Is it a closed vehicle?"

Ford opened the closet to reveal men's clothing hanging neatly inside. "Five minutes till the buggy arrives and it's only partly closed in with canvas. Now tell me about the shooting in your room."

"I woke up to a dead man crashing through the window by the wraparound balcony. I got out fast."

"Did you recognize the man?"

"No." She thought back with a shudder and recalled the wedding ring on his left hand. Another senseless death. A woman would grieve over her husband's inexplicable demise. This morning the man had probably said a casual goodbye, perhaps he'd kissed his wife. They might have even had a small spat as married people often did. Perhaps they'd looked forward to making up this evening—and now he would never return. She blinked back tears, knowing his death, like Grendal's, would always be with her. "Who do you think he was?"

"Probably an innocent bystander in the wrong place at the wrong time."

Suddenly, she recalled more details about the dead man and the blood drained from her face. "From a distance the man would have looked like you. He had dark hair and wore a white shirt and dark pants."

Ford's face remained calm as he hurried to the closet, but his eyes flickered with sorrow and regret. "A change of clothes is in order, but there's nothing here that won't swim on you." He removed a pair of jeans from the closet and held them up to his waist. "Think these will fit?"

Before she responded, he strode into the bathroom

and shut the door. How could he be so calm? Every nerve in her body jangled as if shaken. The Black Rose must have been watching and waiting for a shot. At a distance, the man in her room looked like Ford, but the killer already knew of his mistake since he'd fired again into Ford's room. Was he still out there, waiting?

Ford returned, wearing the jeans, but minus a shirt. "I'll leave money on the bed for what I'm taking." He stuck his head back into the closet. "Wish I could find some shoes. Rubber soles would be better for running."

His broad back had the tanned muscles of a fit swimmer. His smooth skin rippled with a masculine beauty she shouldn't be admiring. When he glanced up and caught her staring, his eyes warmed with a knowing light. She looked away to cover her embarrassment and opened the dresser drawers.

He grabbed a shirt and tried it on, but his broad shoulders didn't fit, and he resorted to putting his white dress shirt and black jacket back on.

While she cracked open the door and checked the hallway, Ford left money on the nightstand. She didn't see or hear anyone nearby, although a crowd had gathered around their former rooms. Ford came up behind her, his warm breath fanning her neck. In the distance, a wailing siren neared.

They walked down a flight of stairs, Ford's arm looped over her shoulders. A bearded man wearing heavy work boots and a plaid shirt lumbered toward them in the narrow hallway. Ford tensed, but kept walking. Her free hand clutched the gun in her purse.

The other man noticed them and tramped by. Two

police officers barreled past, and her nerves jerked in time to the pounding heels of their boots.

She and Ford hurried toward the back exit. Leaving the hotel, they would be the most vulnerable. But perhaps the police presence had forced the Black Rose to retreat.

At the sight of their transportation, Denise's hopes for a clean getaway rose. A sleek black horse in harness grazed on the grass beside the walkway, while the driver stood by the door.

"Bonjour, madame, monsieur."

While Ford gave the driver instructions, she settled into the red leather seat, appreciative of the matching red hood that gave privacy from the sides and rear. "Where did you tell him to take us?"

"Someplace romantic," Ford replied.

As the buggy pulled into the street, he touched her cheek lightly and she frowned at him. How could he think of romance after a man had just been shot outside her room? They were lucky to have survived. As he caressed her neck, sending heated tingles down her spine, she wondered if his sudden affections were a ruse to throw off anyone who might be watching. "This is hardly the time for—"

He drew her against his side. "Relax. We're hidden. I told him to take us into the hills, someplace private. After we arrive we can decide where and how to cross the border and what to do afterward. I think we should head for England and check out the account Gustave gave me and if nothing solid turns up we should return to the States."

"We came here to find the assassin," she protested, unwilling to give up.

"And now the assassin has found us. When I agreed to help you, I didn't anticipate being hunted across Europe. I thought we'd track down your clues and turn the information over to the authorities."

"I'm sorry. My mysterious client got us both into more than I bargained for. But I don't want to give up."

"Just because we go home doesn't mean we're giving up. My power base is in the States. I can fight the assassin better on home ground."

His words made sense. So why did leaving for home feel like defeat and as if she was abandoning her promise to herself to find her cousin's killer? Rhonda deserved more from her than she could ever give in return. Along with despair, guilt snaked through her.

Finding Ford more attractive than she should have caused her forehead to crease, and she edged from beneath his arm. She refused to dwell on her response to his kiss, when she needed to concentrate on finding the assassin. Rhonda's murder couldn't go unpunished.

She bit her lip until it throbbed like her pulse. "You want to give up? Go home?"

For all her determination, not even she could justify proceeding with their investigation. Her shoulders slumped. There was no point in staying. Unless the London bank gave them a name, they had no clues.

At the sadness in Denise's voice, Ford pulled her against his side. "We aren't giving up. I don't command the resources here that I do at home. We need a base of operations. A safe place to gather information and make phone calls without worrying about whether they're being traced. Besides, I could use Martin's help on this.''

"How can your partner help us?''

"Martin is well connected. He graduated from Yale with accounting and business degrees and went on to Harvard Law School with my brother, Max. He has friends in high places, and so do my parents.''

"What's that mean?''

"Martin knows people of influence in business and government. From her charity work, my mother has friends in police departments across the country and in several newspapers, people who could prove useful.''

The carriage driver steered the horse through the busy streets with the dexterity of long practice. She settled against Ford, but tension radiated from her. "Phones in Louisiana can be traced, too.''

"But if anyone tries, we'll know it.'' How ironic they'd come to Europe to hunt the killer who was now hunting them. He forced conviction into his tone, hoping to convince her. "Louisiana is home territory. There, the advantages will be in our favor.''

Sighing, she expelled air slowly. "So how do we go home?''

"As I mentioned earlier, the usual transportation out of town is by bus, train and canal boat. Since we don't have fake identification, renting a car is out of the question.''

She signaled him with her eyes the driver might be listening.

"He doesn't speak English. I asked,'' he reassured her, realizing how little she trusted people.

Momentarily silent, she rubbed her thighs with her

palms, then said, "Ask the driver if there's an airstrip in the area."

He should have thought of that, but the scent of her shampoo and the curve of her hip, distracted him. Actually, she was much more than a distraction. Another woman would have been screaming or crying after a dead body crashed through her window. Not her. After all they'd been through, she refused to give up. He admired her devotion to Rhonda, although he couldn't quite understand it. He'd never understood the cousins' childhood connection. What else hadn't he known about his wife?

Why hadn't he ever realized before that Rhonda had looked to him for approval and happiness? As much as he'd loved his wife, she'd relied on him to make her happy. He'd tried, and mostly succeeded.

His thoughts returned to the woman beside him. He'd never known a woman with Denise's talents, courage and resourcefulness. Her career was clearly important to her, yet she wasn't driven by work, and between crises, seemed able to relax.

More important, Denise didn't seek his approval and that lifted a tremendous weight from his shoulders. Her self-confidence made her an equal partner, and sometimes he enjoyed letting her take the lead. She'd recognized from the beginning that his connections would help them. Where another woman might have felt inadequate or intimidated by his reputation, Denise hadn't hesitated to ask for his assistance. Hell, she'd been fearless enough to kidnap him for it.

She nudged him. "Did the driver say we can fly out of here?"

"Neuchâtel isn't large enough for an airstrip. But

there's a chance we can ride through the Juras to France.''

''I didn't think roads passed through those mountains.'' Denise glanced to the bluish-green mountains ahead, then back to him, a guarded expression in her honey-colored eyes.

''The driver is taking us to a horse farm. For the right price, we can ride straight into France.''

''We'd avoid Customs.'' Her voice rose with excitement. ''We could slip away while the Black Rose is watching the normal routes out of Switzerland. There's only one problem.''

''What's that?''

Her eyes had a sheepish look layered with determination. ''If our survival depends on fleeing on horseback, we're in trouble. I don't know how to ride.''

Chapter Six

"Try and relax. We'll start at a nice, gentle walk. You all set?"

"I guess."

Ford clicked his tongue, and his horse clopped forward with an eager jerk. Denise clasped her arms tighter around his sore chest, and he winced. "You trying to crack my ribs?"

"I'm a city girl. I've never been on a horse."

Ford had spent his summers on a farm. He couldn't remember a time when he couldn't ride. "Red had Max and me riding before we could walk."

"Did you ever fall off?"

"A time or two. Max once fired a shotgun while I rode bareback. The horse stopped dead."

She gripped him even harder. "What happened to you?"

"I went flying over the horse's head."

"You could have been killed."

Riding beside them, Jacques Moran, their guide and owner of their mounts and equipment, didn't say a word. Whipcord lean and bowlegged, he dressed like an American cowboy in pointed boots and jeans, his only concession to his ancestry a beret instead of a ten-gallon hat. He led them away from his Swiss home toward a hard-packed trail over the Juras into France.

Ford had convinced Denise that the best way to avoid detection by the assassin was to avoid the regular routes out of the country. Jacques could take them over the mountains on horseback and he'd agreed to supply them with food, clothing and bedrolls along with the horses. Although she'd never ridden a horse, she'd finally agreed.

Perhaps talking about being thrown off a horse was a mistake. He'd meant to ease her fears while they headed through the pasture. Once they reached the cover of the forest, where a sniper couldn't pick them off so easily, her nerves would settle down. "I didn't get hurt. I broke the fall with my hands and rolled."

The tension eased out of her. "Like a judo throw?"

Obviously he'd hit upon a sport she could relate to. She eased her hold on his ribs and moved with the horse, her breasts rubbing his back. She jerked away, then yielded to the necessity of their closeness. He kept talking to distract her. "You know judo?"

"Mmm."

He'd never known a woman who'd studied judo. He recalled how easily she'd tackled him in the ballroom. He also remembered when he'd pulled the key out of her pocket on the airplane. Suspecting she could have broken away if she'd wanted, he wondered why she hadn't. Her threat to kick the key from his hand probably hadn't been idle. Odd she hadn't mentioned her ability then.

"Excusez-moi, monsieur."

"Yes?"

"The land is flat. We could make better time across this area in a canter."

Denise's fingers clutched him. "Uh-oh."

"A canter is a smooth gait between a trot and a gallop. Just keep your hips centered over the horse's spine. Hold on and don't make any jerky movements."

They'd climbed a bit, the slope so gentle Ford barely noticed. The horses' hooves no longer clopped in hard-packed dirt but landed in muffled thuds in the grass. Few cows grazed here. Instead, sheep and mountain goats roamed amid the high green grasses, while overhead, bluebirds circled lazily.

The horse's swift gait stretched the muscles in Ford's legs still tight from biking. Behind him, Denise bounced. He gave instructions softly. "Move with the horse. Don't fight him."

Twenty minutes later, Ford looked over his shoulder at Denise's face. Her cheeks had flushed to a rosy hue and her eyes sparkled. Tendrils of hair had slipped from her braid and softened her cheekbones.

"We must walk the horses to let them rest. Would you care to try Gilly?" Jacques gestured to the spare horse.

She started to slip off the right side of his horse.

"Other side," Ford told her. "Horses are trained to accept riders mounting and dismounting from the left."

She shifted to the other side and lightly dropped to the ground. Her face turned grim. She pointed down the mountain. "Ford, look."

Below them, Jacques's house, the outbuildings and

cars appeared miniature. But Ford could still make out blue lights atop the cars. Several official-looking vehicles had pulled into the driveway. An explanation to Jacques wasn't necessary since Ford had been up-front with the man before he'd hired him.

Jacques spat into the dirt, his face expressionless. "The police have no reason to come to my home. They must be looking for you."

Clearly, the police had found the body at the hotel and already traced the carriage to Jacques's horse farm. Ford had hoped for a longer head start. "If the police know we came to you, the Black Rose might know, too."

"The cook will say nothing, but I must return or they will be suspicious. I will draw you a map." Jacques cleared a spot in the dirt and drew with a stick. "You must hurry, *oui*. The path through the forest is marked. When you come out, look for a forked tree at one o'clock. Behind the next hill is a cabin. Spend the night there. Do not travel through the night, *monsieur*. The mountain trail is too narrow and the lady is not an experienced rider."

"Who else knows about the cabin?" Ford hated to waste precious minutes talking, but knowing what lay ahead could be essential to their survival.

"The cabin is old, built before the war. Only a few men like myself know. Tonight, feed the horses the grain I have packed and rub them down well. To-morrow, take the northern trail. I will send my brother to meet you. He'll show you the rest of the way and bring back the horses."

Denise mounted Gilly. "Thank you, *monsieur*. We will take good care of your horses."

Ford made a mental note to send the man a breeding stallion after they returned home. Denise's mare
nickered softly and began to follow Jacques.

Ford almost grabbed the reins, but stopped himself.
If they were to survive, she needed to learn to ride.
"Pull back on the reins gently. Turn her without hurt-
ing her mouth."

At first, Denise's touch was so gentle the horse
ignored her command. Slowly she increased the tension until the animal obeyed her. "I think I'm starting
to get the hang of this."

"I knew you'd be a fast learner."

Ford led the packhorse and Denise followed. At
first her horse kept stopping to graze, but she soon
had command over the animal. The forest path rose
gently, angling through pines. The grasses disappeared beneath a forest floor littered with pine needles
and the path widened. She came up beside him, a
defiant gleam in her eyes. "You thought I would
freak about the horse, like I did about being locked
in the dark, didn't you?"

He let her see the surprise on his face. "The
thought never crossed my mind."

"Good. I'm not usually a coward, but I can't seem
to control my fear of being enclosed in dark places."

"So it's not the dark that bothers you?"

She shook her head. "Not unless I'm someplace
where I can't get out."

Sensing she wouldn't have brought up the subject
unless she'd wanted to talk about it, he didn't ask any
questions but let her tell the story in her own way.

She patted Gilly's neck and threaded her fingers

into the animal's mane. "When I was ten years old, Rhonda's parents invited me to Walt Disney World."

"One of the rides frightened you?"

"I loved Disney." She inhaled and released the air slowly. "We stayed at a high-rise hotel. A thunderstorm knocked out the electricity. The backup generators never came on. Rhonda and I were stuck in an elevator. In the dark. I felt as if I couldn't breathe, as if the walls were pressing in on me."

"You two were alone?"

She nodded. "Rhonda's dad was meeting us in the lobby."

"I kept thinking we would fall. Rhonda talked to me until she was hoarse. She held my hand and told me stories about princesses and magic dragons. If she hadn't been there..." Denise shuddered. "I might have gone crazy."

A tightness closed his throat. Rhonda had always been the first person to offer help to a friend. He was glad she'd been there for Denise. No wonder Denise hated being confined in the dark. He couldn't imagine the courage it had taken to leap into the bread truck.

He took her hand, providing what small comfort he could. "If your only phobia is being confined in darkness, I'd say it's a tribute to your courage."

"I wasn't courageous, I endured. Rhonda was the one who kept her head and was so good to me. I always wanted to return the favor, but she never needed me. At last, I've a chance to do something for her." She clenched her free hand into a fist. "I don't want to fail."

"We'll find the Black Rose," he assured her. "I gave up once before for lack of clues. We don't have much now, but we know his calling card, the roses on his victims' pillows. Once we're home, I'll put Martin to work ferreting out information from the CIA and his other government contacts."

"What makes you think he'll succeed?"

"Martin has an extraordinary mind. Once he locks onto an idea, he won't let go. And there's nothing he hasn't solved."

"I hope you're right, but I can't imagine what we may have overlooked. Following the money trail is our best bet. The timing of the deposits from Henschel's account to the Swiss bank can't be coincidence and should lead us to the assassin."

"And Anne is tracking down the growers of the black roses. Maybe she'll have some answers when we reach France."

Denise tilted her head back and peered through the fir trees. "Is the temperature dropping or is it just my imagination?"

"The sun's going down. I'll unpack a jacket." He halted his horse, climbed down and approached the packhorse. Finding the jackets in the saddlebags under the slicker, he handed her the smaller one, then donned the other before remounting.

"I'd like to arrive at the cabin before nightfall. Are you up for a trot?"

"That's like a fast walk?"

"A little bumpier. Keep your heels down." He led the way, knowing her horse would match the pace. Over his shoulder, he caught her biting her lip in determination as Gilly trotted after him.

They broke out of the forest about twenty minutes later. He stopped and surveyed the view. In the direction of one o'clock, he spotted Jacques's forked tree. They had another hill to cross before they reached the cabin.

A dark cloud scudded toward them, partially blocking the setting sun. In the distance, ragged edges of black clouds lay over the isolated hills and tumbled down the craggy gray slopes. Shifting gusts of wind buffeted the clouds, casting shadows over the rock-laden valley below.

Ford reached for the slickers. "We'd better put these on before we're drenched."

She took the one he offered her, pulled the rain-hood over her head and tied the drawstring under her chin in a cute little bow. The yellow slicker draped her like a cape, with slits for her hands to hold the reins. "If we're going to get wet, we might as well be moving forward."

The storm held off longer than he'd expected. They'd almost reached the forked tree before the heavens split open, sluicing them with icy rain. The gray hillside turned to slick brown mud, and the horses worked to drag their hooves through the sucking goo.

Thunder rolled across the valley with a dragon-size gust of wind that flapped a corner of Denise's slicker. Spooked, Gilly reared, nostrils flaring. Wide-eyed, Denise lost the reins and threw her arms around the horse's neck. Ford swore, twisted to grab her reins and missed.

Her mount crashed down on all four hooves, splashing water and mud in Ford's eyes, momentarily blinding him. The wind snapped her slicker once more. Gilly snorted and broke into a terrified gallop.

By the time Ford's vision cleared, her horse was half-way across the rock-studded hillside, and his heart hammered his ribs at the right of her on the runaway horse. Denise clung to the animal's rain-slick back. But how long could she hold on?

AT BREAKNECK SPEED, the horse's powerful hind-quarters bunched and released, hurling woman and beast over a jagged outcropping of rock. The jarring landing rattled Denise's teeth, cut off the scream in her throat.

Wind swept back her hood. Needles of rain pounded her back and sneaked under her slicker until her clothes stuck like paste. With numbed fingers, she clutched the horse's mane, one thought reverberating in her head.

Keep your heels down.

She wedged both feet in the stirrups and prayed Gilly wouldn't pitch her onto the sharp rocks. She desperately needed to regain control, but she dared not release the mane to grab the dangling reins.

As she ducked under a branch, the horse swerved and skidded in the mud. Denise tilted to one side and clenched the mare's slippery neck to remain astride. Gilly stumbled, but the game horse didn't go down. Denise's sore rump and leg muscles shrieked for relief, but she held on.

Lightning flashed ahead, and the zigzagging bright-ness lit up the hillside like fireworks. Gilly halted straight-legged, flinging Denise forward. The pommel gouged her side, chasing from her lungs what little breath she had left. Only her death grip around Gilly's neck prevented a fall onto the rocks.

Throbbing pain from the pommel jerked her upright.

They'd stopped.

The horse's head drooped with fatigue, and rain ran down her back and neck in rivulets. The animal's sides heaved, and she sidestepped, nervously avoiding the rocks.

Fighting the agony in her side, Denise bent and retrieved the reins. The movement seared fire from her hip to her backbone. She closed her eyes until she gained control of the pain.

Swaying, she reopened her eyes, forced herself to look around. She saw no sign of the forked tree, Ford or the cabin. She had no idea where the runaway horse had taken her or even if she'd crossed the border into France. Darkness had fallen, leaving her in blackness except for the occasional lightning bolt.

If the assassin caught her now, she'd be helpless except for her gun.

Her gun!

Fumbling with the saddlebag, she slipped her hand inside, gripped cold metal and yanked out the weapon. After taking the gun off safety, she chambered a bullet.

"Steady, girl," she said to Gilly.

Mustering all the strength in her legs and arm to hold the horse firm, she waited for a break in the thunder, pulled the trigger twice in quick succession. The echo of the shots were puny compared to nature's cacophony. Gilly trembled but didn't so much as raise her head.

Let Ford hear my signal.

Denise counted to one hundred and fired the last

shell. Closed her eyes. Drifted in and out of consciousness.

SHE OPENED HER EYES to the sight of the tanned cords of Ford's neck, and the feel of a pulsing heartbeat against her cheek. She sat crosswise on the saddle with her head tucked beneath Ford's slicker, his strong arms around her waist, his pleasant male scent embracing her. Drowsy and exhausted, she shut her eyes and rocked back to sleep.

The next time she woke, she found herself staring at the ceiling beams of a pine-scented cabin. Rain plunked and pattered against the roof and wind whistled around the corners and seeped through the cracks. Inside, the cabin was dry and cozy. A fire crackled in a woodstove. An oil lamp cast a circle of light and only the corners of the room remained dark. She couldn't see Ford, but his wet shirt hung over the stove, dripping into a rusty frying pan. Wrapped in a blanket, she lay on a sleeping bag on the floor, a dry jacket pillowing her head.

She was naked.

Ford must have stripped off her wet clothes before placing her under the blankets. While she couldn't fault his first aid, she felt decidedly uneasy about his seeing her body.

How could she be worried about Ford's opinion as if she had no other concerns? she admonished herself. By now, the police and the Black Rose must know where they were headed. They had to leave tomorrow to beat the assassin to an airport. And she was in no shape to ride. Just turning her head caused pains to shoot down her side to her hip. Fire radiated from her tender side and her legs cramped. The hours of cold had stiffened the muscles, and at the slightest movement, she had to grit her teeth to hold back a groan.

Suddenly, the door burst open and a gust of wind and rain blew in with Ford. Shirtless, he kicked the door shut, strode to the stove and stacked the armful of wood he'd carried inside, then rubbed his hands in front of the fire.

Firelight reflected off his glistening chest, highlighting his toned muscles with red, gold and orange. Water trickled over his hard face and sculpted cheekbones, down the strong lines of his neck. Soaked jeans clung to his muscular thighs and slim hips like steam to a mirror. As if feeling her gaze, he twisted until his eyes captured hers with a fierce possessiveness. "How do you feel?"

"Just peachy," she croaked, her words barely audible.

While her response brought a flicker of admiration to his eyes, his face remained grim. "I saw the bruises. Don't try to move."

He didn't have to worry. She rested her head on her folded jacket and watched him pour water from a canteen into a cup. He'd brought the saddlebags inside and draped her clothes over a chair beside the stove.

Ford approached, kneeled beside her and lifted her head. The blanket slipped from her neck to her collarbone. At his closeness, the pounding of her heart was so strong she couldn't believe he didn't hear it. She greedily sipped from the cup, wondering how her throat could be so parched after her thorough drenching. A shiver racked her.

"Are you cold?" His voice registered concern as he pulled the blanket back up to her chin and tucked the edges around her.

"Maybe a little." Grateful to be inside and dry, she refused to complain, but she had to fight to keep her teeth from chattering. "Where are the horses?"

"In a shed out back. I fed them and rubbed them down." With an unreadable expression, he set the cup beside her and returned to the fire. "I'd never have found you if you hadn't fired those shots. It's amazing you stayed on Gilly." The admiration in his tone warmed her.

"I remembered you telling me to keep my heels down."

After loading the stove with wood, he returned and offered her more water. Again she drank and the blanket slipped a little. Ford's gaze didn't leave her face. How far would the blanket have to go before he noticed? "You carried me here."

"Yes."

"You undressed me." She stared directly into his eyes, seeing wariness vie with something else, something she would have called desire on the face of another man.

"Yes."

He didn't defend his actions. Didn't explain. Didn't ask if she'd understood the reason he'd removed her clothes. His bold glance held hers without apology. "There's something I've been meaning to tell you."

Her lips went dry. *Here it comes.* The comment that would shred her fantasies, where he'd make some crack about sharing body heat. The comment that would reduce Ford to regular-guy status. The comment that would help her to resist his charm.

"We make a good team."

If she'd still been drinking, she'd have sputtered water all over. Instead, she choked back a coughing attack at his unexpected words. Was he talking about their working together or something else? Different interpretations formed in her head as she stared at his hard-hewn face. His cryptic statement revived his earlier advice on what to say if she was unsure how to respond. "Really?"

His sonorous voice rang with sincerity. "For a while there, I thought I'd lost you. I'm glad you're okay." He touched her shoulder. Fickle nerve endings registered a tingle dancing down her arm. His touch affecting her was a bad sign.

A good feeling.

Warmed to her toes by his slight caress, she suddenly felt too hot under the blanket. His fingers traced a path up her neck and his thumb stroked the line of her pulse, sparking and firing tantalizing sensations.

Assigning any special meaning to his gesture was a fool's game. *He's just being kind. He would do the same for any woman.* A glance into those steady blue eyes told her he'd recognized her response. With his fingers skimming her pulse, he'd known exactly how his touch aroused her. He'd missed nothing—neither her instinctive response nor her effort to hide it. His preoccupied expression told her he was factoring in this new knowledge about her, deciding how to proceed. She'd inadvertently given him an advantage she couldn't regain.

Although inexperienced with men, she was no fool.

Now that he knew how she'd respond to his slightest touch, he could guess the depth of her feelings. Despite every effort, she couldn't banish her feelings about him. Instead, she'd enhanced budding emotions with solid memories of the heat of his muscular chest, the strawberry taste of his kiss, the afterglow from his gentle embrace.

She loved him, but she'd never admit her feelings. She wasn't what he wanted. He'd told her he wouldn't try to replace Rhonda again. She had no reason to believe otherwise. Ford was a hard man, but a man of his word.

If she gave in to her trembling need, what would her future hold? No doubt she'd be better off keeping her pride and pretending her love didn't exist. Yet, the idea of shamelessly seizing the moment and creating memories to last a lifetime tempted her.

Before she could decide whether to yank off the blanket or pull it to her chin, Ford rose and veered toward the saddlebags. "How about dinner? You'll feel better with food in you."

He'd given her a reprieve. Time to decide. But her mind spun in confusion. Without tasting, she chewed and swallowed the sandwich he gave her. She usually knew her mind, but she couldn't put her whirling thoughts in order.

He sat close by, stoking the fire between bites of food. The silence between them had a hot, sharp tension that hadn't been there before. She wished he'd say something. Anything.

He stared at the fire, his expression inscrutable. Several locks of dark hair spilled over his face. He needed a shave, but she found the shadow on his jaw darkly appealing. He pulled off his boots and socks, then set them by the fire to dry. From his purposeful search of the saddlebags, she guessed he'd come to a decision.

He pulled out a small jar. Watching her, his blue eyes almost black in the shadows, he twisted the lid and sniffed. "We have to ride out of here tomorrow."

"I know." Every muscle in her body ached. Experience with severe bruising told her tomorrow she'd be even stiffer. Her bottom was sore, but the bruise on her hip worse. But they had to keep moving to reach an airport before the Black Rose outflanked them. Somehow she'd manage to ride. "Did Jacques pack pain pills?"

Ford shook his head. "Not so much as an aspirin."

The strong spicy aroma of liniment filled the room. He approached, crowding her a little. "I rubbed down the horses. Now I'll do the same for you."

"I'm not a horse."

"I noticed." He stared long and hard, his lips curled in a sensual grin, and his eyes lit with a challenging energy. Her damn nerves leaped until she braced herself to prevent a tremor. If his slightest touch drove her wild, how was she going to stand a massage?

As if unaware of her turmoil, he casually picked up the jar of balm. "This will help you heal, keep you from hurting. A massage will relax your muscles, and you'll feel better."

He seemed to be giving her a choice, but she didn't want to cope with the sensory overload of a massage. Resisting him would be almost impossible if he touched her. At the thought of his long fingers rubbing salve into her muscles, she fought back a tremor. "But—"

"You're in no condition to refuse." His tone hardened. "Now turn over while I hold the blanket."

She bit her lip, knowing he was right. A massage wasn't sexual foreplay. Her body was demanding relief from injury. Although no bones were broken, her legs cramped into severe knots. "I'm not sure I can move."

He lifted the blanket but held it between them, giving her privacy. "Take your time. Turn toward your good hip."

As she moved, the agony seared her side. Her face beaded with sweat. Despite her cramping legs, the weakness in her arms and the groan of misery she couldn't hold back, she finally flipped onto her stomach with an unladylike grunt.

Ford replaced the blanket over her. "Are your ribs hurting any worse?"

"I don't think so." She relaxed as the stabbing hot ache receded. Despite a bruise caused by the pommel, now that she'd turned over, lying on her stomach was more comfortable.

"Good." He stoked the fire and settled close to her side. "I'm folding the blanket to your waist, okay?"

His question was rhetorical because he pulled the blanket back before she consented. Cool air lapped her back. She was lying without a thread of clothing, and she had no doubt he would look his fill. And then he would touch her. Exposed, she felt more vulnerable than she ever had. And sexier.

Ford gathered her hair and twisted it over one shoulder. Just his fingertips on her neck caused her to quiver in expectation. Warmth stirred inside her, and she held her breath in anticipation of his first touch.

The jar scraped the floor, and his hands rubbed together. "Tell me if you get cold."

He had yet to touch her, but her skin heated from the palpable energy radiating off him. Dizzy with the effort of hiding her reaction, she was grateful he couldn't see her face and the effect of his hands on her.

She squeezed her eyes shut. How had she gotten into a situation where she felt so helpless? Usually she had more sense. Usually she held tough. But Ford had a way of twisting her into snarls until she ended up fighting her own resolve. If she spent too much time around him, she'd end up a quivering mass of raw indecision.

He used both hands on her neck and shoulders, finding and rubbing the tensed muscles of her collarbone. The sharp tangy aroma of liniment relaxed her while it lubricated the friction of his hands. With strong fingers, he massaged in sure, even strokes. She'd had no doubt he would be an expert masseur and she wasn't disappointed. He homed in on the sore spots like sonar.

His thumb feathered over her neck with a lightness that made her want to do something embarrassing, like moan or squirm, and triggered fantasies entirely too graphic. He was all-business, while, fuzzy and light-headed, she drifted in a pleasant haze, and her stomach clenched tighter.

"Relax. Let me know if I'm too hard on you."

He worked her neck and shoulders until the tension drained, his firm caress so delicious, she never wanted him to stop. He moved his hands in hypnotic, yet terribly stimulating, circles. He proceeded down her back, his thumbs digging into the hollow between her shoulder blades, loosening the upper joints and gradually circling downward. She almost relaxed, until hit by a sudden suspicion. ''Ford, how far are you going?''

''No more than you want. No more than you need,'' he murmured in a husky tone.

What the hell was *that* supposed to mean? Her pulse fluttered in unaccustomed panic. Making love with Ford could never be casual for her, and to allow him to proceed when he didn't return her love would devastate her. Yet her body refused to listen, vibrating with a humming femininity she'd denied too long.

As he dug his knuckles into the base of her spine, brushing closer and closer to the blanket, she resisted the urge to clench her fists. She gritted her teeth to hold back a moan of pleasure.

As devil-may-care as if stripping a bed, he pulled the blanket over her bottom and down her legs. Cool air met sore flesh. The heat from her blush flared hot enough to warm the room.

His thumbs dug into the small of her back and the heel of his palms found the crests of her backside. He moved slowly, working the soreness from the muscles in efficient strokes, kneading her bottom, chasing the stiffness away.

''You've got a great butt, round, firm and muscular beneath.'' His deep voice simmered with barely checked passion. ''I've been admiring you since I took the key out of your pocket.''

Relishing the combination of heat and desire in his

tone, she concentrated on the pleasure he was giving her. She'd never realized how powerful touching could be. His palms curved to her flesh and the only thing on her mind was what he might do next.

His hands felt so good. He moved to the tops of her thighs, dangerously close to rendering the massage much more personal. Anticipation kindled in her tummy.

How far was he going? How far was she willing to let him go? Her blood was singing, but Ford continued to knead in a most professional manner. Was the man made of granite?

He worked down her legs with the cool efficiency of a robot. Another man might have covered her up. Not Ford. Irritated that naked she apparently didn't tempt him, she wished she could read his thoughts. His breathing was a bit jagged, but from exertion? Or arousal?

Although she didn't dare, she wondered what he would do if she rolled onto her back and held out her arms.

"Turn over."

As he spoke her thoughts aloud, her stomach flipped a triple somersault. "Excuse me?"

"It's time to turn over so I can do your front."

"I don't think that's a good idea."

"That bruise on your hip needs tending."

"Ford, I'm naked." And a virgin—no match for his experience.

"I know you're naked. I undressed you, and you're not a sight I'm likely to forget," he said with admiration and a bit of impatience. "I've already seen you, all of you."

That was supposed to make a difference?

While she'd lain on her stomach, the evidence of her arousal was hidden. But if she turned over, he would read the anticipation in her taut nipples and swelling breasts, the quiver of her belly, and see her nostrils flare with a shortness of breath. Worst of all, he might suspect the yearning in her aching heart.

All too humiliating when deep down she expected rejection.

One glance over her shoulder into Ford's approving eyes made her feel more like a woman than she'd thought possible. She'd waited so long for the right man, she'd begun to think she was incapable of love. Now she knew better. But the only man she'd ever wanted would never love her back and all she would have was this memory. Oh, he might make love to her now with the same wonderful passion with which he did everything else. But later he would return to a life where she didn't fit in.

Damn. Why did she have to want him? Why did only he have the ability to warm her soul?

She didn't even have the excuse of her injuries. As painful as the cramps had been earlier, he'd worked out the spasms and charley horse, leaving only minor soreness.

If she didn't take this opportunity, if she spared herself from hurt, she'd regret her cowardice the rest of her life. The possibility existed that neither of them would live to make it back home. While she was torn by indecision, flirty little sensations in her breasts urged her to let him do as he pleased.

A discordant excitement swept through her. Her nerves hummed and tingled and tightened.

The scrape on the floor indicating he'd picked up the liniment rattled her more than the clash of thunder outside. She visualized his strong fingers dipping into the cream, spreading it over her breasts, giving pleasure.

He rubbed his palms back and forth, warming the liniment. His touch would be gentle, exquisite. "Denise? Turn over."

Her mind said *no.*

Her body said *yes.*

Her heart said, *I don't know.*

"Denise?"

Chapter Seven

Firelight flickered over Denise's silky-soft, supple skin. Her flesh had danced beneath Ford's hands, making him yearn to learn every inch of her by touch. She'd been designed for pleasing a man. For pleasing him.

As she quivered beneath his fingers, he sucked in his breath. She had wonderfully voluptuous breasts, broad shoulders and hips and a tiny, sexy waist. Her wild, willful hair was thick and curly enough for a man to lose himself in. And her legs were gorgeous, lean and toned, and long enough to wrap around him and give as much as she got.

Desire, hot and hard, filled his loins until his jeans grew tight. He'd never thought a woman's body could be so beautiful. He'd never known a woman so courageous. To find both attributes in one woman made his heart pound with a savage yearning.

He could no longer touch her to give comfort, to ease the stiffness from her muscles. He wanted to touch her the way a man touches a woman. But did she want him?

When he'd spoken her name, a quiver had twitched

down her back and had him biting back a groan of satisfaction that she'd responded to just the sound of his voice. When his hands had stroked her, he'd felt the wildness of her pulse, but was it desire? Or fear?

He'd been thankful at first that she didn't know she was turning him on. When she'd turned and looked at him, he'd thought about shifting his position so she could see the effect she was having on him. But as he'd worked out the stiffness in her muscles and assessed the physical battering she'd taken, he'd realized she wasn't up to making love. She needed to heal.

Restraining himself from sweet seduction, he bent and pulled the blanket over her. She turned to her good side, her eyes, full of questions, boldly locking gazes with his. The prolonged eye contact gave him his answer—not the one he wanted.

She would refuse him.

"I'm not about to make love with you." Her voice was raspy with regret, yet threaded with fierce pride.

"Are you hurting?"

"The charley horse is gone. I'm much better, thanks. But I won't—"

"Why?" That her refusal had nothing to do with her bruises aroused his curiosity, stunned and disheartened him. He knew she wanted him. She'd reacted to his lightest touch. Deep in his heart, he suspected she was not only rejecting him for tonight but was about to reject him forever. Torn between smashing his fist into a wall and shaking an explanation out of her, he fought to understand. Even now her pupils were dilated with arousal. So why was she refusing him?

"Because you're Rhonda's husband."

Ford rocked back on his heels, flabbergasted. Her normally logical thinking had gone haywire. "Rhonda's gone."

"It doesn't seem right to take advantage of her death."

Ford bit back his temper. "Rhonda was good and kind and wanted the best for everyone she knew. She would want us to go on with our lives."

"I know you're right." Denise shook her head. "But knowing doesn't stop my guilt. A fling would be like a slap in the face to Rhonda's memory."

While her words rang with the truth, he sensed there was more she wasn't saying. Much more. What was she holding back? She hid behind memories of Rhonda, and he lashed out, his temper hot. "A fling? Is that how you think of me?"

She met his temper with a calm voice but her eyes were eloquent with hurt and accusation. "*You* told me you'd never again try to replace Rhonda. What am I supposed to think except that your capability to love died with Rhonda?"

Her words got through and ripped his gut. He swore under his breath, raked a hand through his hair and paced the confines of the cabin, wishing the storm would abate. He hadn't thought this through. He was in Europe to avenge the woman he loved, not dally with her cousin, and they had to ride out of here tomorrow with their minds sharp. The assassin would likely meet them somewhere along the way. Now wasn't the time to face his past, so he smothered his anger and ignored the hollow spot love once filled.

He'd rather run himself into exhaustion than face Denise's disturbing question.

Damn it to hell! She was right.

Denise wasn't the kind of woman a man took to bed for one night. She deserved to be loved and cherished for a lifetime. No matter how attractive he found her, how much his arms ached to hold her, she deserved more than he had to give. He'd given all his love to Rhonda and his ability to love had died with her.

Denise awaited an answer, but he had none to give. He removed the oil lamp from the nail on the wall, turned off the flame and set it within easy reach. In darkness, he shucked his damp jeans, hung them to dry and slipped into a sleeping bag.

Lying on his back, hands laced behind his head, he stared at the ceiling. The howling of the wind matched his dark mood. For the past months an empty numbness had separated him from the world like a gauze shroud. He'd operated on instinct, submerging the grief with days overloaded with work and nights at glittery social functions that held no meaning.

Now he was alone with his thoughts. And Denise. Facing either wasn't easy. An uncomfortable silence fell between them. She shifted, rustling the blanket on the sleeping bag. He should apologize, not for wanting her, but for not wanting her enough. But he couldn't think of the right words. "I don't know what to say to make things right."

"Words can't always fix things," she said in a choked voice.

"We can't go back to the way we were before tonight, can we?"

"I can pretend, if you like," she offered, sounding more composed than he would have wished. "Once we get home, we'll both go our different ways."

"I want you to stay at my house until the Black Rose is captured. I have a good alarm system. I'll hire bodyguards. And I'll replace every window with bullet-proof glass."

"I don't—"

"You can have your own room." He wouldn't let her refuse. "I'm hardly ever there. You won't see me often."

"But—"

He wasn't beyond using dirty tricks to protect her. He played his trump card. "Rhonda would want me to keep you safe."

She released a frustrated sigh. "Do you always win?"

"Usually." Her rejection was too fresh in his mind for him to turn cocky.

"Ford, tell me something. During the past months, were there any attempts on your life before we came to Switzerland?"

"No. Why?" His tone rose, letting her know he'd caught on to her change in subject.

"According to the maid, a black rose was left on your pillow. If the assassin had a contract to kill you and Rhonda both, why didn't he make another attempt at you?"

"I don't know. Dr. Henschel hired the assassin so we wouldn't learn the fertility clinic had accidentally planted Rhonda's egg in Brooke's sister, Nicole. He knew if we found out Rhonda's child had been born and raised by another woman, the clinic would have come under intense investigation. With outside scrutiny, Henschel's scheme of overbilling patients would have come to light and his career would have been washed down the tubes. He couldn't risk finding out because, as a member of the clinic's board, I'd have both personal and business reasons to go after him. After Henschel was caught trying to cover his nefarious schemes, the assassin might have gone to ground.''

She remained silent for a moment. ''The Black Rose had forgotten about you until we came nosing around. These attempts on your life are my fault. I should never have kidnapped you, forced you to help me.''

''That's ridiculous!'' She couldn't hold herself responsible for putting him at risk. ''I could have ordered my pilot to turn around at any time. I wanted to come. I'm only sorry you're now in danger, too.''

The danger had forced him into facing his past and thinking about the future. With her kidnapping of him, Denise had accomplished what his marriage to Lindsay could never have done. Denise intrigued him and by doing so, he felt renewed, as if he'd come back to life. Sure, he'd worked hard and forced himself to date during the past months. But none of his business successes or personal relationships had meant much. Then Denise had come along and his reactions were spiced with a new zest.

He could just make out her silhouette. She rested on her side, her head on her palm. ''How do you know Dr. Henschel hired the Black Rose because of the mixed-up eggs?''

He frowned. ''What do you mean? Why else would

Henschel have hired a killer to come after Rhonda and me?''

"I don't know. It just seems odd that the assassin stopped pursuing you. Perhaps the primary target was Rhonda."

He shook his head. "That's not possible. Besides the fact that Rhonda didn't have any enemies, I was more capable of ruining Henschel's reputation than my wife."

"You did a marvelous job keeping most of this out of the newspapers."

"That was Mom's doing."

"Eva sounds like an unusual woman. We met briefly at Rhonda's funeral. I recall her as slender, youthful and down-to-earth."

"Mother's looks are deceptive. There's a steel mind under her fragile looks. Her IQ is in the genius range, and if she thinks her family is in danger, she defends us with the ferocity of an enraged lioness. But when it came to Rhonda's killer, even Eva was stumped. Everyone involved in the scandal at the Kine Clinic is dead. Although I'm on the board of directors and had access to all the records, they didn't leave many, if any, clues behind."

He'd given up the search to find the assassin once before when he'd reached a dead end. But then he hadn't Denise's skills to help him. She hadn't lied about her instincts. She had a knack for finding what the other professionals he'd hired had overlooked, discovering Grendal, the black roses and the transfer of large sums of money from Henschel's account to Switzerland. What was the connection?

This time, with Denise's help, he wouldn't give up.

He, too, owed Rhonda. His resolve to continue the investigation had nothing to do with giving him more time to spend with Denise. Did it?

"Rhonda's daughter now lives with your brother and his wife, right?" Denise's thoughts obviously had taken a different direction.

"Brooke has raised Skye since she was a baby. She's a great mother and she adores Skye."

"You didn't want to raise her?" she asked softly.

Want to raise Rhonda's daughter? He worked past the sudden lump in his throat. The room shifted, swam before the excess moisture in his eyes. Assuming the responsibility for Skye would have been a blessing that might have eased his loss of Rhonda. He'd ached to shower Skye with the love of a father, but for the child's sake, he'd settled for the role of doting uncle.

"Rhonda would never have separated her daughter from the woman who'd raised her. Brooke is the only mother Skye's ever known. I think Rhonda would be pleased." And he'd accepted his fate. "Besides, Max is Skye's father."

"What?"

Her surprise stabbed him, piercing deeper with each word he revealed next. "We kept this out of the papers, too. I contracted the mumps when I was a kid. Dr. Henschel at the Kine clinic told me I can't have children. Since Max and I are identical twins, we have identical DNA. He supplied the sperm to impregnate my wife. In the mix-up, Skye was implanted in Brooke's sister."

His admission stirred unbidden tumultuous regret at what could never be. A family. Children. Grandchildren. He forced down the sorrow and doubts. His life had taken another path.

As if sensing his pain, Denise changed the subject. "Brooke's sister and her husband died in a car accident, right?"

He nodded. He had to give her credit for doing her homework. But the fact that she didn't seem to care that he couldn't have children interested him more. But why should she care about his inability to create a family when he'd told her he would never replace Rhonda? Besides, she might not want children. Anything was possible.

"Dr. Henschel killed himself before you could find out for certain who he'd hired to assassinate you?"

"Yes. Henschel had a personal vendetta against me. He'd expected to be promoted to my position on the board at the Kine clinic. He resented when Norton Industries bought the clinic and I took the seat he'd wanted on the board of directors. That's when he started stealing from the patients. So you see, it's more likely I was the real target."

"Perhaps you're right."

He could tell by her tone that she didn't believe his theory of the assassin's going to ground after Henschel was caught by the police. But he had no reason to think otherwise.

Her voice slowed as her breathing evened. "If I'm to stay at your house, I'd like permission to go through Rhonda's personal papers. Yours, too."

"Sure." Her interest pleased him. He had nothing to hide, and he had lots of papers. That way, he could keep a close eye on her.

DAMN IT! The Black Rose wasn't supposed to make mistakes. Killing the Swiss man on the woman's balcony was unprofessional, at best. At worst, it could lead to capture by riled authorities.

Of course, after the mistake, the Black Rose had outsmarted the Swiss gendarmes, hiding among the townspeople like a chameleon. But meanwhile, the prey had slipped away undetected. Either Ford and Denise had crossed the Juras into France or doubled back to investigate. He'd never expected such cunning from Ford. But no matter the man's shrewdness, the Black Rose would pick up their trail as soon as they surfaced.

And finish them off.

THEY RODE OUT the next morning after a breakfast of thick crusty bread, cheese and strong coffee. Denise would have enjoyed the ride more if she could have banished her worry that the assassin might ambush them as they exited the mountains. While she didn't dwell on the problem, she couldn't put the thought entirely from her mind.

Last night's rains had left the ground wet, and the horses' hooves plopped in the mud. The air held a clean scent of pine, and as the sun rose, she removed her jacket. They came across a tree downed by lightning, its trunk crushing the bushes beneath it, and she realized how lucky she'd been to survive the storm.

With Ford riding ahead, her gaze was drawn to him as if he were a finely sculpted piece of art. His disheveled white shirt had several stains and a few rips, but a little muss couldn't detract from the square set of his broad shoulders or his thick, silky black hair.

As the path turned, she glimpsed his profile, the high forehead, the straight nose and strong chin, and she realized what a magnificent specimen of man he was. For a moment, she regretted they hadn't made love.

He rode as if he were part of the animal. Although Ford owned businesses that spanned the globe and was no doubt accustomed to luxury hotels, he had no difficulty roughing it. He'd lit the woodstove and heated coffee as if he was unacquainted with servants waiting on his slightest whim. She couldn't imagine him being out of place anywhere.

He'd been wrong about one thing, though. They didn't make a good team. Sure, he could fit into her world just fine. But she couldn't make the same journey into his. And with the memory of Rhonda always between them, she had no reason to try.

After several hours of riding, she stopped her horse in the shadows of thick brush that hid them from below and looked out over the sweeping vista of rock-strewn grass mixed with patches of forest. Far in the distance, she could just make out several farms amid dazzling mustard fields and rich pastures.

She glanced at Ford, immediately noting the tense angle of his jaw. "What's wrong?"

Eyes squinting into the sunlight, he pointed to a knoll that lay between them and one of the French villages far below. "A rider just crossed that hill."

"I don't see anyone."

"He's climbing through the tree line on the ridge."

Her nerves tingled, but she didn't feel the usual sensation of warning at the back of her neck that signaled danger. "Jacques did say he'd send his brother to meet us. But let's ride in the cover of the trees until we see who's out there.''

"It'll take longer, but I'd rather play it safe."

She focused on the ridgeline. "Have any ammunition left?"

Twisting in his saddle, Ford pulled out a handful of shells. He loaded both weapons, dividing the bullets between them. After checking the safety, he handed back her gun. "We each have five shots."

Ford slipped the gun into the waistband of his jeans and veered into the woods, pulling the packhorse behind. In silence, she followed, wondering if she would ever feel safe again. She'd never been hunted before. Never worried that a professional assassin could pick her off from over a mile's distance and she'd have no warning.

That they'd kept moving had no doubt worked to their advantage. Sometime this morning they'd crossed the border from Switzerland to France. If they were lucky, they'd find transportation to Paris and catch a plane home. If their luck ran out, they would die on this mountain, and then she'd regret that she'd resisted making love with Ford last night.

But if they survived, she'd made the right decision. She'd refrained from taking advantage of Rhonda's death. And she'd protected her heart from the eventual anguish of separation from a man who, no matter how appealing, couldn't love her.

Ford halted the animals and put his fingers to his lips. He withdrew his gun and she followed suit.

Through the pine needles, the faint clop of a horse's hooves approached. Ford leaned close, lips inches from her ear, his coffee-scented breath fanning her face. "Let him pass by before we notify him of our presence."

She nodded, her mouth dry. How would they know if the rider was Jacques's brother or the assassin? She didn't voice her concern since the rider was almost upon them. When she heard the man whistling, she sighed in relief and lowered her weapon. No assassin would be so noisy.

As the horse and rider passed, she peeked around Ford. Smaller than his brother, Jacques, the Frenchman wore jeans with protective leather leggings. His brown-and-red-plaid shirt matched a brown cap. But one glimpse at his shock of white hair and light blue eyes in the same shade as his brother's and she couldn't doubt his identity.

Apparently drawing the same conclusion, Ford returned the gun to his waistband. *"Bonjour, monsieur."*

The whistling ceased and the man whipped his head around in surprise. A broad smile revealed a missing front tooth. *"Bonjour.* I am glad to see you. I am Bernard Moran. You spent the night in the cabin and did not get too wet, *oui?"*

She'd been expecting Jacques's brother to be younger, but Bernard's face was even more wrinkled and weather-beaten than Jacques's. She'd bet he was close to eighty. Unlike his thin brother, Bernard had a potbelly that jiggled with his mount's every step.

"Jacques explained you needed me to lead you out of the mountains."

BERNARD LEFT THEM in Beaune at the bus station. There had been no sign of the assassin, but now that they were back in civilization, she couldn't help looking around nervously. The empty bus station eased her concerns. No one seemed interested in rumpled American tourists.

"Come on." Ford took her hand and steered her toward several phones. "I need to make a call."

"Wait just a minute." She tugged on his hand and pulled him to a halt. "I thought we'd agreed. No phone calls."

His eyes flickered with impatience. "I agreed to *discuss* it with you first. The chance of the Black Rose tracing the call from here is nil. At this time of day, I'll have to call my secretary at home, so unless the Black Rose has tapped Anne's personal phone line, I'd bet a phone call is safe."

He sure made good arguments and the confidence radiating off him in waves kept her from arguing. No wonder he was so successful. "I agree it's fairly safe."

He raised an eyebrow, reached for the phone, and dialed. "Anne, sorry to wake you in the middle of the night."

Meanwhile she made a few calls of her own, checking on black roses.

Twenty minutes later he hung up, a pensive expression in his eyes. "Anne called the American Rose Society. No wholesaler or breeder sells black roses."

"Breeder?"

"People who grow roses are called breeders." A bus raced by, blowing her hair, and she ran a hand through her locks. "I was hoping black roses would be rare so they would be easier to trace. I never expected the flowers to be almost nonexistent."

"Grendal could ! ve made a mistake. Maybe the flowers she found on Rhonda's and my pillows weren't black roses."

"I wish we'd taken the petal we found at Grendal's house. We could have had it analyzed."

Ford frowned. "Don't forget the British ambassador, Bruce Willowby, told us about other assassinations where black roses were left on pillows. And now the rose society says black roses don't exist?"

"I've done some research. Apparently, roses come in lots of colors, but mostly shades of reds, yellow, orange and white. Green ones are scarce. Black roses must be genetically engineered."

"The rose society gave Anne the name of one breeder of black roses, a woman in Amsterdam named Yvonne Jansen." Ford checked his watch and steered her toward a bus that had just rolled into the parking area. "If the blacks are that rare, we might find the assassin's address in this Yvonne Jansen's customer files."

She glimpsed a matching excitement in the tension of his neck that set her heart pounding. She kept her voice calm. "Should we go see her?"

"I vote we make a side trip to Amsterdam before we head to London to trace Henschel's payment to the assassin."

"We could call Yvonne, instead."

He shook his head. "She might talk to us by phone, but I doubt she'll turn over her customer files to strangers. A visit in person would be better."

He was taking charge again, swaying her with the merit of his argument. "How far is Amsterdam?"

"Several hours by car from Paris."

Her hopes rose, but the last few days had taught her caution. "What about crossing the border?"

"We won't have to worry. It's like driving a major highway."

He curved an arm over her shoulder and drew her to him. After last night, she should have been uncomfortable, but leaning against him seemed as natural as changing their plans. "You'll love Amsterdam at this time of year." His voice, deep and sensual, reminded her that they lived in two different worlds, but the knowledge didn't dampen her enthusiasm. If Yvonne could tell them who her customers were, they would have a trail to follow.

"We'll fly from Amsterdam to London. I'd planned to be gone another few days. But I must be back in New Orleans in time for the annual stockholders' meeting of Norton Industries."

"Problems at home?" He was arranging their schedule without consulting her. Since she had no reason to object, she didn't protest.

He followed her onto the bus. "Nothing I can't handle. A new holographic imaging process in Silicon Valley looks promising, and I want in on the ground floor. But I can afford a side trip."

Just because he could take time to divert their journey to Amsterdam didn't mean going was a wise decision. She'd thought she could control her feelings for him, but instead of diminishing, her love was growing, and she suspected she was heading for unimaginable anguish when the time came for him to leave her.

She shoved her feelings aside as she took the window seat. "Ford, do you suppose someone doesn't want you to make that meeting?"

"And that someone hired the Black Rose?" He considered her suggestion as he settled next to her. "It's possible. Someone has been buying Norton Industries stock from many different sources. A hostile takeover could be in progress. If I miss the meeting, it would shake stockholder confidence."

"But?" she prodded, sensing he'd already dismissed her suggestion.

"But the Black Rose tried to kill me months ago. And we're almost sure Dr. Henschel paid the assassin. I can't see how the Black Rose could be connected to my missing this meeting."

"You're probably right."

But her instincts said otherwise. Why was the Black Rose suddenly trying to fulfill an old contract? When they returned, she intended to look into those stock purchases.

But first, they had to survive in the Black Rose's territory. Once they questioned the grower, word of their whereabouts might leak out, making it imperative for them to find the Black Rose before he found them.

Chapter Eight

Denise looked out the window and watched the countryside pass. The autumn leaves were just beginning to turn from green to gold and russet. A barefoot woman waddled along the roadside carrying a chicken in a cage. Children raced by on bikes. They passed vineyards and stopped in small towns of pink-roofed houses, tree-lined streets and medieval churches with stained-glass windows. But her mind was not on the scenery.

Ford sat beside her, cool, calm, confident. He was every inch the highly successful international businessman. While he'd spoken to his secretary, she'd been reminded the past few days were not real life, but merely an interlude between business deals. The tender man who'd massaged away her soreness couldn't disguise the self-made millionaire who wined and dined presidents and kings.

His automatically assuming control set him apart from her. While his aura of command was attractive, his demeanor isolated him, making her wonder if the gap between their views of the world was too wide to bridge. When other men would show hesitation,

Ford was already off and running with an assertive drive that led to his lightning success.

Yet she feared his approach to romance was also one of conquest. She wasn't a trophy to be won and then placed on a shelf as an accessory to any man's life. She had to be an integral part of him and doubted Ford's ability to let her into his heart.

It was late afternoon when they arrived in the heart of Paris. They disembarked and walked onto the crowded street. Ford seemed at home amid the broad boulevards crammed with traffic. Chic pedestrians wearing the latest in high fashion strolled past sidewalk cafés. Bistros with wooden fronts painted either brown or dark red called out to her rumbling stomach with their scent of garlic and onions sizzling in butter, and beef simmering in huge steaming pots.

The city fascinated her but she felt so exposed. She'd never spot a tail in the crowd, never spy a gun aimed at them. The sooner they left the streets, the less chance they'd have of being spotted, and the safer they'd be.

"Ford, I'm not sure we should hire additional protection."

"Why?"

"Extra people will slow us down and draw attention to us. In addition, calling in security agents might tip off the assassin to our whereabouts."

"We'll be back in another day or two," he agreed. "I guess we can wait until then."

Hoping she hadn't given him bad advice, she glanced back over her shoulder. Nothing suspicious struck her. Her neck didn't itch.

"Where are we going?" she asked, hurrying to keep up with his long-legged stride.

"To my apartment."

Her surprise that he owned property here didn't stop her from tugging his arm. "Just because we haven't seen the Black Rose doesn't mean it's safe to return to your former haunts."

"Norton Industries owns the property. My companies keep places like this all over the world. We use them for visiting dignitaries, salespeople, wholesale buyers. I seldom come here, so we should be safe."

She walked beside him, curious about the secretive glimmer in his eyes. "How do you know the apartment's unoccupied?"

"Anne arranged for the present visitors to stay at Relais et Châteaux, a prestigious chain of converted châteaus and manor houses."

Ford suddenly turned through an arched wooden trellis covered with climbing ivy. A stone path led them through a miniature garden to elaborate glass doors trimmed with brass. Reaching into a mailbox on a stone wall, he plucked out a key.

"If I were a thief, that is the first place I'd look for a key," she chided.

After unlocking the dead bolt, he opened the door for her in a sweeping gesture. "But would you know the code that turns off the elevator alarm?"

The foyer boasted a marble floor, lush plants and framed art. She didn't know what she'd been expecting, but the profuse display of wealth made her uneasy. "You have your own private elevator?"

He gestured for her to enter. *"Mais oui, mademoiselle."*

When the elevator opened along one wall of a vast living room, her breath caught. Her entire house would fit inside this one room. Floor-to-ceiling windows dominated one wall that overlooked a park. Chandeliers dripped gleaming crystals and sent prisms of light dancing across papered walls and antique furniture. Thick white carpet warmed the room.

A telephone answering machine's light blinked, and Ford pressed the button. A woman's pleasant voice spoke, "I hope you find the arrangements satisfactory. A week's worth of clothes for you and Denise are hanging in the closets. Cash is in the safe. Let me know if you need anything else."

She spun around in confusion. When had he made these arrangements? "Who was that?"

"My secretary, Anne."

He'd arranged a place for them to stay and clothes without her knowledge. "But she's in New Orleans. How could she have...? When did you...?"

While she attempted to verbalize the jumble of questions in her mind, Ford unbuttoned his shirt. "Anne assumed if I was in France, I'd be heading to Paris."

"You didn't—"

He carried a portable phone from a table, clearly about to make more arrangements without discussing them with her. Her frustration level rose as he sat beside her and spoke so reasonably, "I didn't mention where we would be staying. But she knew we were in France and heading to Amsterdam. Paris is a logical stopover. Anne is good at anticipating my needs."

I'll just bet she is.

"How could she know my clothing size?" Denise was stunned by how quickly he'd taken charge and how fast her jealousy had flared.

"Anne's resourceful. She probably called my mother to find out your size. She did see you at Rhonda's funeral." Ford reached for the phone and dialed. "I'll order dinner in. Why don't you see what Anne picked out. She has marvelous taste in clothes."

Annoyed at hearing how wonderful Anne was, frustrated that he sought to be rid of her by suggesting she look at clothing while he arranged their every move, she plucked the phone from Ford and canceled his call. "How old is Anne?"

He cocked his head to the side. "Jealous?"

"You know her home phone number."

"I also know the restaurant's number where I was ordering dinner. Does that mean I'm enamored of the cook?"

"Are you?"

"Well, I may adore Chez George's *côte de boeuf* but I haven't asked George to marry me." Ford's gaze dropped to her hips. "He doesn't have the curves I adore on a woman."

He would not tease her out of her jealousy. Besides, their lives might depend on whether Anne was trustworthy. "Tell me about Anne."

"I already have. She's a wonderful organizer, loyal, punctual and a spectacular researcher. She has stunning brown eyes, soulful, really, and she adores me."

"Ford?"

"What else could a man want—"

"You've never seen me toss a two-hundred-pound man across a room, have you?"

"—in a sixty-five-year-old secretary?"

"Sixty-five?" she squeaked, feeling every bit the fool.

"That's what she admits to. I suspect she's pushing seventy-five." He raised an eyebrow at her expression and took the phone back. "Now can I call for dinner? Or would you prefer to throw me across the room?"

She groaned and stomped toward the bedroom in disgust at herself.

"By the way," he continued, teasing her as he dialed, "after you do the throwing, do you end up on top?"

She marched into the first bedroom and slammed the door behind her. How could she have been so dumb? Just because she loved him didn't mean she had to wear her feelings on her sleeve. And it hadn't been very nice of him to tease her, either.

It would have served him right if she'd tossed him onto that seductively thick carpet and put him into a headlock until he begged for mercy. She kicked the antique bedpost and grimaced. She had to rein herself in. It was one thing to pine for Ford at a distance, quite another to control herself when she'd spent most of the day with him pressed hip to hip. She was a normal woman with normal needs. If she couldn't help responding to a good-looking hunk—

Oh, stop it. Who do you think you're kidding?

Plopping onto the bed, she stared at the frescoed ceiling. She'd admired Ford since Rhonda had brought his picture to the college dorm. And while this jaunt was to find Rhonda's killer, the reality was different. In their short time together, Ford had imprinted his scent, branded his touch and seared his kiss into her soul. He'd spoiled her for other men.

It was one thing if she couldn't have him, and she might hate herself for her jealousy, but selfishly, she didn't want anyone else to have him, either.

"Knock, knock."

"Go away."

He opened the door and marched into the room, a smile lingering on his lips, his shirt still unbuttoned to the waist.

She scowled at him. "I could have been changing."

"That would have been delightful." His eyes twinkled. "I enjoy looking at you, especially your—"

She wanted to hit him. "Did you come in here to torment me or do you have a purpose?"

"Dinner will arrive in an hour. I'm sorry I couldn't take you out for our one night in Paris, but we can make it memorable. I thought we could dress up and pretend we are someplace fancy. Do the clothes fit?"

"I haven't looked," she said, feeling churlish. Why did he have to be nice when she wanted to pick a fight? It was almost as if he knew she was trying to distance herself from him and her feelings for him with anger, but he was refusing to allow her to do so.

Muttering something under his breath, he strode to the closet and swept back a mirrored door, revealing more fancy dresses than she'd wear in a decade. He reached inside and pulled out a red dress with a halter-style neckline that tapered to the waist and a flirty skirt that would barely cover her thighs.

With an appreciative whistle, he hung the dress on a hook on the door. "Ah, yes. You'll look nifty in this." He bent and retrieved matching four-inch red heels, set them below the dress and gestured to the dresser. "I'm sure there are suitable underthings, but I'd prefer you wore nothing at all beneath the red dress."

"You must be the most outrageous man in France—make that Europe." She swore at herself for letting him see her fit of jealousy. No matter how romantic her feelings, it was humiliating to think he knew that he'd reduced her to a puddle of hormones. "You march in here and expect me to wear what you tell me to?"

He seared her with a look so hot it stole the air from her lungs. "Wear whatever you like. Wondering what you have decided will lend an air of mystery to the evening."

The pillow she threw just missed him on the way out. He chuckled. Insufferable, overbearing man.

Just imagining herself in that red dress twisted her stomach into trembling tangles of emotion. The garment would emphasize her every curve. If she wore that dress, she'd feel sexy, assured and desirable. She ached to wear it. For once in her life, she wanted the beautiful feelings inside her to be reflected on the outside for a man she loved. She wanted to revel in his admiration. She wanted to be wanted by Ford.

But he didn't love her.

While she'd enjoyed weaving the fantasy of a night of lovemaking in his arms, reality had a way of catching up with her. Giving in to her feelings might be disastrous. Once she went to him in that dress, there would be no turning back.

She rose from the bed and walked over to the closet door. As she fingered the red material, a pain squeezed her heart.

FORD SPENT THE TIME waiting for her to dress, imagining her in red, wondering what she'd wear beneath the garment. As he poured himself a glass of wine, he was unable to resist envisioning her moving with an underlying sensuality...warm...soft...enticing. She'd join him, focusing her tawny eyes, tentative and suggestive, on him with longing. It was her eyes particularly—in her expressive, lively face that drew him.

When she entered the den finally, there was a long moment of silence. She wore a slithery floor-length gown. A black gown.

While she met his eyes with her chin raised in defiance, a heaviness of disappointment settled in his chest. Although disconcerted by her clear-cut rejection, he relied on good manners to see him through this setback.

"Would you like a glass of wine?"

"Yes, please."

All through dinner, he wondered why she so stubbornly refused what was growing between them. He'd seen the passion flirting in her eyes, heard the throaty undertone of sensuality in her voice, felt the air vibrating with a tension that could only be caused by a mutual attraction.

She wanted him. He recognized the signs—could

see, feel and smell the intoxicating blend of female response. He couldn't doubt the signals she sent. She was ready. The thin excuses she'd given him at the cabin about feeling guilty over enjoying herself at Rhonda's expense wouldn't wash. Rhonda would have wanted them to grab whatever happiness they could find. He knew that in his heart, and he suspected Denise did, too.

Realizing Rhonda would approve had made him reconsider his decision not to make love to Denise if he couldn't give her all the love she deserved. He now realized he yearned for more than one or two nights with her. He wanted to explore every inch of her body, but more important, he ached to know her most intimate thoughts. He wanted to know about her ideas on a thousand silly and serious things. She'd aroused his curiosity, intrigued him, taunted him. To discover if he had deeper feelings, he needed to deepen their relationship. And what better way to do that than by making love?

He wasn't a patient man. Yet he vowed to be patient.

He would continue to let her know he wanted her, touch her every chance he could. To break through her stubbornness, when he didn't know what caused it, wouldn't be easy, but Ford was always up for a challenge. He looked forward to kindling the sparks in her eyes into a bursting white heat. If she made love with the same passion she did everything else, the reward would likely be a complete meltdown.

Some moments were worth waiting for. Some women were worth waiting for. And deep in his heart, he knew Denise was one of those women.

THE DISAPPOINTMENT OF last night was already fading during their drive to Amsterdam the next day. He consoled himself that someday he would take her back to Paris and they would do the town.

While he drove the company car, leaving Paris behind, Denise drummed her fingers on her lap.

"What is it?" he asked.

She sighed and a slight shudder rippled through her. "If the Black Rose is motivated by money, why is he still after you? Dr. Henschel is dead and can't pay for a completed contract."

"Maybe the Black Rose thinks we know more than we do. Maybe he doesn't like us on his trail."

She slumped in the seat. "Or maybe he's a psychopath out to finish what he started."

For a time, they lapsed into silence. At the sight of the Dutch farmland with its picturesque windmill-dotted landscape, Denise had relaxed. Even he felt a certain peace stealing over him as they drove by the canals with their water gates then past a late-Gothic cathedral.

She bit her lip, frowning over the Dutch map, while he drove toward Yvonne Jansen's rose-breeding farm. He noticed circles under her eyes. Denise couldn't have slept much last night. Fighting the pull between them, along with the subtle pressure he was applying, would eventually wear her down. He wished he could make the decision easier for her, but she'd repeatedly refused to discuss their situation.

She looked up from her map. "Take the next right onto Schraeder, then another onto Rieveld. Do you think Yvonne speaks English?"

"The Dutch I've known are fine linguists, and almost everyone speaks at least some English, especially in the larger cities and tourist areas. If Yvonne enters her roses in international shows, she'll probably be fluent in English. If not, I only know a smattering of Dutch, and we'll have to return with a translator.''

"How many languages do you speak?"

"Not so many when you consider many Europeans speak four or five." He paused for a moment, then said, "Besides English, French and Spanish I'm working on Japanese. I do a lot of business in Asia."

She sighed. "I feel culturally deficient speaking just one language."

He wished he could tell her she was in no way deficient. Nature had gifted her with a bounty to be enjoyed.

But he kept his thoughts and his hands to himself, answering as if the conversation fascinated him as much as what she wanted to keep hidden. "Until now, you've had no need to know another language."

She pointed to a brick driveway in front of what appeared to be a combination home and office. "This is Yvonne Jansen's address. Pull in over there." The gabled house was a hodgepodge of architectural styles. Its stone walls appeared medieval, while other parts of the construction were obviously early twentieth century with a few modern conveniences thrown into the charming mixture.

The immaculate front yard consisted of neatly trimmed shrubs, flower beds and borders underplanted with herbs that laced the air with the spicy, exotic scents of thyme, rosemary and dill. Bare canes arched over a low fence, surrounded a mailbox and cascaded by a tumbling waterfall that bubbled pleasantly. Although none of the roses were in bloom, the landscaped area revealed a love of gardening.

Denise's eyes brightened with excitement as they approached the arched office door. "Isn't this yard lovely?"

He ducked under a wind chime and pressed the doorbell. As they'd driven to the farm, he'd noted the extensive greenhouses out back, the windmills pumping water to irrigate the flowers and the state-of-the-art alarm systems that protected the property. "I'll bet the grounds are spectacular when the roses are in bloom."

Steady footsteps clicked against wood as someone approached. The door swung open to reveal a tall woman in her early fifties with a lanky frame. Her brown eyes, her best feature, looked at them from a somewhat narrow face. She had a button nose and a small mouth, all devoid of makeup, and she wore her nut-brown hair in an artless braid. In contrast to Paris's sophisticated and polished women, she was dressed in a frowsy white blouse and threadbare skirt.

"Yvonne Jansen?" he asked. She seemed young to have developed such an extensive and prosperous business.

"*Ja.*" She bent and scooped a fluffy white cat into her arms.

"Do you speak English, Miss Jansen?" This time Ford put more friendliness into his voice.

"It's Mrs. Jansen." Her thin eyebrows came together in a befuddled frown as she stroked the cat's neck. "Please don't tell me I've forgotten a sales call? I am not dressed to receive—"

"We don't have an appointment," Denise interrupted. "But we have come a long way to see your roses."

"My roses?" Yvonne's face softened and her lips broke into a smile.

"I want to stock a rose garden and we'd like to see your selection," Ford said.

The woman stepped back and opened the door for them to proceed inside. "Come in, please. I should warn you, once I start talking about my roses, I go on and on."

"Is anyone else here?" Ford asked, looking around curiously.

"I run this business alone. I am a widow."

"I'm sorry," he murmured.

"My husband left me these wonderful roses to keep me from the loneliness."

Still carrying the cat, she led them down a dark paneled hallway into a bright and spacious office with curving glass windows that caught the light. Bouquets of roses in a variety of pinks, purples and yellows filled vases. Baskets of rose plants hung from the ceiling while ceramic pots displayed miniature flowers in delicate pink and soft lavender.

Eyes sparkling, Denise took in the room with an appreciative sniff. "This is your office. You work here?"

Yvonne set down the cat, led them to a window seat and gestured to a desk almost covered by flowerpots. "These plants are my special projects. I'm still budding some of my roses. But fall is the best time to take cuttings."

Denise took a seat beside Ford. "Cuttings?"

"That's how we rose breeders propagate our plants. Did you not come here to buy?" She lifted a pot and set the plant on the table before them.

Ford didn't answer her question. "Do you keep records of your buyers? I'd like some references."

"Of course. I have mailing lists and a catalog, all produced on my computer." She drew herself up proudly while the cat rubbed her ankles. "Ach, I am forgetting my manners. Would you like some tea or coffee?"

"No, thank you," Ford said. "We came here because we'd heard you grow black roses."

"*La fleur du mort.* The death flower. It is very rare, the blacks are my proudest possession. Roses grow in every color except blue. Now that I have the black, blue is my next great project, very difficult."

His hopes rose. If black roses were this rare, she couldn't have grown many. They need only check a limited number of buyers. "Do you have a list of customers who have bought black roses from you?"

"I do not sell the black roses."

Denise's eyes rounded. "Never?"

"I cannot grow enough blacks to sell. The temperature must be just right, the hormone balance perfect. In addition, the plant requires sixteen essential nutrients, and if any are missing, it will not grow or bloom."

"Could we see the blacks?" Denise asked.

"I'm so sorry. They are not in bloom. You must come back in the spring."

Denise gestured to the blooms around them. "How did you make these others bloom out of season?"

"Ah, most roses are more cooperative than the

black. I can change the temperature in the green-houses and adjust the lighting and fool them into believing it is spring." She frowned. "The blacks are stubborn. I have not learned how to fool them."

"Have you given away any of the blacks?" Ford asked.

"No." Anger flashed across her face. "But six or seven years ago, just after I finished at university, thieves broke into my greenhouse and stole cuttings from my blacks and a rare green. I spent much money to put in the alarm system."

Denise looked at Ford who was obviously as puzzled as she. The Black Rose had killed Rhonda during the winter. How could the blacks only bloom in the spring? "Does anyone else display blacks at the rose shows?"

"*Ja*. Sir Richard Kaplan has mastered the black rose. But I do not think he stole the cuttings. A man in his position would not stoop to thievery. Besides, his black roses are different from mine."

"How so?"

"Roses come in six shapes and five flower centers. My blacks are shaped high-centered like this yellow." She plucked a stem and pointed to the petals. "See, the long, inner petals of the bud arrange themselves in a pointed cone. This shape is often found in hybrid teas, grandifloras and floribunda."

Denise stared at the yellow rose. "And Kaplan's blacks?"

"Are quarter-centered." Yvonne picked a lavender flower and handed it to Denise. "See the inner petals fold into three, four or five distinct sections. It is different than mine. And so is the shape."

Denise twirled the rose between her fingers. "Does Kaplan sell his black roses?"

"I do not know. He probably doesn't sell many. Why must you buy black roses? I have many other—"

"I'm sorry," Ford spoke gently. "You've been very helpful. But we are only interested in the blacks because of their uniqueness."

"Then why are you here?"

"I'd hoped you could sell them to me. But I appreciate your time. Would you by chance have Kaplan's phone number and address? Maybe he'll sell them.

After repositioning several potted plants from her desk, Yvonne slipped in front of her computer. She typed quickly, bringing up a database. "Here he is, Sir Richard Kaplan, and his London address." She printed the information on a piece of paper and handed it to Ford. "Will you go there next?"

"Maybe, why?"

"English rose breeders tend to be secretive about their stock. They are often reluctant to share information with outsiders."

"We appreciate your help," Denise said.

"Thank you." Denise shook Yvonne Jansen's hand. "You've been terrific."

Denise and Ford said goodbye and walked back through the garden to the car. Ford opened her door for her. "I need to get to a phone."

"Why?"

"To make plane reservations. If the timing works out, we can be in London tomorrow, then fly home the following day."

She waited until he walked around the car and slid behind the wheel before saying more. "Ford, when did Ambassador Willowby say the Black Rose began leaving the flowers on his victims' pillows?"

"At least twelve years, maybe fifteen ago."

"And how old would you guess Yvonne Jansen is?"

"About thirty."

"So unless she took up the job of a professional assassin at the age of fifteen, she's not who we're looking for."

Ford started the car, made a U-turn and headed back toward the city. "You think Kaplan is the source of the black roses?"

"We can't forget the stolen cuttings," Denise said. "Or the fact the money was wired to London."

"Let's see what background information Anne can dig up on Sir Kaplan." He gave her his best charming glance. "Are your instincts warning you of trouble?"

"Nope. It's my normal paranoia kicking into gear."

Chapter Nine

Ford followed the signs to downtown Amsterdam. Preoccupied with her thoughts, she was surprised when Ford pulled into a parking lot. She sure hoped he intended to eat soon. Her stomach rumbled at the very idea of food. But as they walked around the block, instead of entering a restaurant, he led her into an electronics store filled with television, stereo and computer equipment.

Now what was he up to? "What are we doing here?"

"I can't work effectively unless I'm in constant communication with my office. This is the best electronics store in Amsterdam."

She should have realized he needed to be in touch with the world. Ford couldn't maintain control if he wasn't on top of things.

"Excuse me," Ford said to a bored-looking clerk with a handlebar mustache and a pierced eyebrow. "I'm looking for a satellite phone system."

Satellite meant wireless. She doubted most hackers would have equipment sophisticated enough to track that kind of system—if one existed, and if he could buy one in Amsterdam.

The salesman twisted one end of his mustache and spoke in a disinterested monotone. "The microCOM-M transceiver is about the size of a notebook computer and uses an antenna that folds like a handheld fan to make and receive calls, faxes or E-mail via Inmarsat-M global telecommunications."

"It feeds through orbiting satellites?" she asked, trying to decipher his technobabble into comprehensible English.

Ford nodded. "The system makes some use of land-based phone networks, but with this baby, we can call from anywhere in the world. The phone runs on AC or DC and offers secure-talk options."

The salesman eyed Ford with suspicion. "We just stocked that system last week. How do you know so much about it?"

She recognized the confident look on Ford's face and whispered, "Don't tell me. You own a company that makes it, right?"

"Guilty." He turned to the salesman and handed him a credit card. "No need for the box."

She waited for the clerk to leave and ring up the sale before protesting. "Ford, if you use the card, the transaction can be traced."

"Relax. We'll be leaving the country within the hour."

"I suppose dinner is out of the question?" she grumbled as they walked back to the car.

He took her hand, squeezed and held it. "Not at all. What would you like?"

The scent of apples and cinnamon wafted out of a restaurant, and she tried to steer him toward the inviting scent. "That smells delicious."

He kept going, tugging her back to his side and handing her the car keys. "First, I have to make a few phone calls. Would you mind driving?"

She sighed with resignation, ignoring her protesting stomach. "Where to?"

"The airport."

While she navigated the foreign streets of Amsterdam, plagued by the city's concentric ring of canals, one-way streets and traffic, he flipped on the operating system and placed call after call, secure in the knowledge that the satellite system couldn't be traced.

"From Amsterdam, I'd like two first-class tickets to Rome, two to Capetown, another set to Buenos Aires, another to Tokyo and two to London. That's correct, all in the same name. All leaving within the next hour." He glanced at his watch and spoke to Denise. "That leaves us thirty minutes to get to the airport with another half hour to spare."

Finally she understood. He'd cleverly masked their destination by purchasing multiple tickets to different countries. If the assassin tried to find them by computer, the Black Rose would have no idea which flight they'd taken. The tickets cost a fortune, but Ford didn't seem to consider the expense. It must be nice.... She'd converted the price of guilders to American currency and figured he'd paid almost eight thousand dollars for the phone system—but to him that was probably pocket change.

She followed a sign that pointed toward Schiphol Airport while Ford woke Anne with another phone call. Poor woman.

"Sorry to wake you. You can reach me by phone and fax now. I've E-mailed the numbers to the office.

I need you to do more digging. I want everything on Sir Richard Kaplan, business interests, hobbies, his travel itinerary for the past decade or so. The same information is needed on Yvonne—oh, you already have it? Great. Fax it to me from work.''

Ford listened for a minute. ''Don't worry. I'll be back for the stockholders' meeting. Yes, we're heading to London. I'll need a car at the airport, more conservative clothing for both of us and a place to stay the night. Make us an appointment with Kaplan. Don't tell him why I'm visiting. That's right. I'll also need a suitable gift, business cards, the entire British package.'' He paused again. ''Good idea. Call them and give them my love. Thanks, Anne. I owe you one.''

Ford's lips tightened at something Anne said, he hung up and immediately began dialing. ''Martin, yeah, I know it's the middle of the night. Sorry. Have you learned who is buying Norton Industries stock?'' He paused. ''Keep on it. I don't want surprises at the stockholders' meeting. I'll be there. Count on it.''

Denise waited, impatient for him to finish. She wished she could do the background search on Kaplan. She only hoped Anne was as thorough and trustworthy as Ford thought.

''Beef up security,'' Ford ordered. ''Don't hire any new people. I'd prefer to keep this in-house. I'll authorize overtime. Have the phones checked for taps, the offices for bugs. I'm not sure when I'm returning yet. How's the buyout coming on the Silicon Valley deal? Don't lose that, the technology is impressive. Sell our interest in the railroad stock if you need the cash. Put a limo at my disposal and have a maintenance crew reinstall the windows in both my home and the office with bullet-proof glass. Yes, I know it'll cost. Thanks.''

Realizing the powerful man beside her was the *real* Ford Braddack, she wondered where the man who'd enjoyed a simple meal on horseback had gone. He couldn't be easily categorized, and both sides of him were all too compelling. While the man on horseback made a great partner, she wasn't as sure about the man beside her.

She pulled into airport parking just as he ended the conversation with Martin. His partner didn't sound as eager to buy the new technology as Ford. But then, she supposed that's what made a great partnership, complementing one another's strengths. ''Where now?''

''I need to place one more call.''

''You'd better hurry,'' she said, barely containing her irritation.

He checked his watch. ''Relax. We have thirty minutes and carry-on luggage.''

Ford switched to French, and she had no idea who he was talking to. At this point, she didn't care. Just the speed of his conversation depressed her.

Not true.

His pace had nothing to do with her melancholy. While the calls might be necessary, she took exception to them. He needed to communicate with his office, but she missed his glances that indicated he cared about her opinion. He hadn't discussed his plans with her. He'd ordered transportation, clothing and accommodations as if she was someone to be taken care of—not a partner.

She missed his touch and the feeling of closeness they'd shared, but she missed being treated as an equal more. She couldn't stop wanting Ford's love. Although she couldn't do anything about his feelings, she could put an end to his high-handedness.

Instead of allowing him to make all the decisions while she sat cooling her heels, she'd see to feeding her growling stomach. Without waiting for him to finish his conversation, she tossed him the keys and opened the car door, looking for signs to the terminal.

She hadn't taken five steps, before he joined her and took her hand. He glanced sideways at her. "What's wrong?"

"I'm hungry." Spotting an elevator, she kept moving and maintained a breezy tone. "While you work, I thought I'd find us something to eat before the flight."

He released her hand and curled his arm across her shoulders. "I've taken care of a meal."

"How did you know what I wanted to eat?"

Something in her tone must have warned him her question wasn't about food. They entered the elevator and he pushed a button, his eyes piercing hers with honest confusion. "Tell me what's bothering you. Please."

"I am capable of choosing my own food and clothes. When possible, I'd like to be at least consulted before you make decisions that affect me."

At her impassioned words, he straightened, his affable manner hidden by a guarded yet intimidating wariness. "I see."

A momentary flicker in his eyes revealed her words had wounded him before he hid the vulnerability behind a polished reserve. After a long, disconcerting moment, she ducked from beneath his arm and faced him. "I know you mean well, but I'm not used to someone making decisions for me."

He set his newly acquired satellite system on the floor. "You never mentioned this before."

Reaching out with one long finger, he pressed the emergency stop button, halting the elevator between floors. Images flashed across her mind, of Ford carrying her through the rain, of his hands on her backside during that massage, of the heat in his eyes when he asked her to wear the red dress.

As she recognized that look, the same look he had before he kissed her last, her breath caught. Fire spiraled deep in her belly. Her legs weakened and she swayed. She retreated until her back pressed the cool wall. "I don't like being bossed around. That's one of the reasons I started my own business."

He stalked her, stopping mere inches away. "You aren't very good at following directions. The red dress would have looked great on you."

"I wanted you to back off."

"You don't know what you want."

He stepped so close that with every breath, she could feel heat radiating off him, smell the hot spicy scent that made her mouth water. A tremor of desire shook her.

Damn him, he knew how she felt. Without words, he could elicit a response from her traitorous body until she'd almost forgotten her argument.

If he hadn't noticed her response, she might have stood a chance of convincing him she didn't want him. But he'd seen her tremble, heard her catch her breath. She couldn't fight him anymore.

She reached around his neck, dug her fingers into his hair and pulled his head down to kiss her. She leaned closer, molding her body to his. They kissed. She had no idea for how long they tasted each other, sensually exploring with tongue and lips and roving hands. She only knew she wanted him to hold her, kiss her like this forever.

She grew hotter, needier. Her senses spun, yet he seemed in complete command. Except the bulge in his jeans told her differently. And so did the catch of his breath.

He was the one who pulled back, his eyebrow raised. "You picked one helluva time to change your mind."

"I didn't..." Heat rose to her face. He'd turned her mind to mush, her body to a tingling mass of raw nerves. What was it about his kisses that made straight thinking impossible?

He grinned, clearly pleased with himself and her admission that he could overwhelm her so easily. She'd gone from downright annoyance to practically ready-to-rip-his-clothes-off in less than an instant. He'd be intolerably confident now.

As he pushed a button and the elevator resumed moving, her nervousness turned to apprehension. She'd always prided herself on her independence. She had her own business and no one would decide what she should eat and wear—no matter how well-intended his choices. Just then, the doors opened and she walked beside him, her thoughts pensive and so-bering. How could she feel so wondrously happy and so terribly miserable at the same time? If this was love, she wanted no part of it.

As if she had a choice.

She was so jittery after their encounter in the elevator, her hunger had disappeared. When they were in danger, he tried to protect her, yet treated her as an equal. But once the immediate peril had passed, Ford took charge with an ease so smooth and deceptive she had difficulty recognizing where to draw the line.

Ford picked up their tickets at the Dutch equivalent of the VIP counter, and she waited impatiently for him to return. If she wasn't careful, she'd be moping around, waiting for his next smile, his next pat of affection.

Loving him might be easy, but she didn't find it uplifting. She was too selfish. She wanted him to love her back.

If he couldn't, she didn't want him at all.

Unfortunately, her body had other ideas. When he held her and kissed her, she couldn't resist the warm sensations that overloaded her circuits and melted her resolve as if he'd wired a conditioned response to her every nerve. It wouldn't be easy sitting beside him on the plane while she yearned for his kisses.

Get a grip. Easier said than done. She simply couldn't ignore him and she couldn't leave him, either. Not yet.

SO THEY'D GONE to Amsterdam, then London. Let them. The Black Rose should have known Ford, the quintessential businessman would pick up the money trail and follow it like a bloodhound on the scent. But it didn't matter since the Black Rose wouldn't be making more mistakes. He now knew Ford's destination. He knew where Ford was vulnerable.

The assassin would be waiting.

AS THEIR TAXI PULLED to a stop in front of Sir Richard Kaplan's office building, Ford saw Denise's gaze sweep Charing Cross, looking for anyone suspicious. Beneath open umbrellas, the crowds hurried to and from the underground and the bright red double-decker buses that led to every part of London. Denise barely spared a glance at the narrow-fronted stone and brick buildings with their cluster of chimney pots across the roofs. Never letting down her guard, she was busy eyeing a tourist entering the National Gallery.

Their stop at the Bank of England earlier had proven their enemy was smarter than they'd anticipated. Although they hadn't been followed, the money hadn't been withdrawn from the bank either. The sight of messengers in traditional pink tailcoats and scarlet waistcoats couldn't banish their disappointment of learning the funds had been transferred out of the bank. Ford had hired a specialist to follow the trail which could lead to many more banks in different countries. Clearly the Black Rose had anticipated they might seek out his identity by tracking the payments.

Ford vowed patience. Sooner or later the money would be withdrawn from a bank and a name would be on the account with a signature. Someone would have seen something. Someone would remember.

In the meantime, Kaplan waited for them. Ford

paid the taxi driver and opened an umbrella for Denise. She grimaced at the rain. "What reason are we giving Kaplan for our visit?"

"According to Anne's fax, his family owns a consortium of businesses throughout Europe. His interests range from glass factories outside Venice to the Djakarta spice trade. He's seventy-three years old—an unlikely assassin. I think honesty is our best bet."

"Okay."

He was pleased by her willingness to compromise. With her nose pressed to the taxi window, she'd seemed more interested in their fog-filled surroundings than conversation. Not that he blamed her. He'd been preoccupied with business. Although he'd planned to be on a honeymoon with Lindsay right now, he'd never intended to be out of touch.

Their driver stopped before a six-story building with the firm's name painted in discreet gold leaf on the front door. Denise's practiced eye picked out the video cameras above the door and surveyed the doorman with a billy club at his side.

A secretary buzzed them inside Kaplan's office. A brawny man in an immaculate business suit stood to greet them, his sharp brown eyes enigmatic. Although his stomach possessed a paunch, there was nothing soft about him. The man moved so smoothly, so effortlessly, he scarcely seemed to expend any energy at all.

After introductions that included an exchange of business cards, Kaplan's secretary offered them tea, which they all refused. The office interior was cool, decorated in eighteenth-century antiques, depicting an old-world elegance without a computer or fax-modem in sight.

Ford extended a bottle of Scotch, a private label almost impossible to buy at any price. "Please accept this as a sincere thank-you for seeing us on such short notice."

"Thank you." Kaplan accepted the gift with a thoughtful nod. "How may I help you?"

"I—" Beside him Denise stiffened. "We," Ford amended, "came to ask you about black roses."

Kaplan laced his fingers together on his desk. "The Black Rose. A fitting name for your wife's killer."

Although Ford wasn't surprised at the man's knowledge, beside him, Denise tensed. Businesspeople of his caliber didn't walk into meetings without having done some research. He expected Kaplan to have a file on his net worth, his businesses, perhaps some information on Rhonda's death. But not even he had expected the man to connect the Black Rose with Rhonda's death.

"You've heard about the Black Rose?" Denise asked, clearly using all her inner strength to ask only one question at a time.

"Only a very little."

The Englishman had a flair for understatement. He had already admitted knowing more than Interpol. Ford took Denise's hand, hoping Kaplan's information might lead them to the assassin. "We would be grateful for whatever you can tell us."

Kaplan nodded to his secretary. Silently, she left.

"Because I developed a black rose for my garden, my son vividly recalls his encounter with the assassin."

Denise squeezed Ford's hand tightly and Ford caught every nuance of her action. They'd come too far, gone through too much not to hunt down every lead. Grendal was to have identified the assassin and since her death, they'd been unable to dig up a name or a description of the Black Rose. Identifying the killer would be the first step in apprehending him. With Rhonda's killer behind bars, she could rest in peace and he could have his life back.

Ford kept his voice soft but firm. "Any information would be a great help to us. This meeting will remain confidential. We will not endanger your son."

The two men's stares locked. Ford knew better than to offer this man payment. Money would be an insult if Kaplan believed his son might be endangered for telling what he knew.

Tension grew in the ensuing silence. Kaplan stared into Ford's eyes so long, the man had time to read his soul. Ford held Kaplan's gaze, withstood the scrutiny, letting him see the smoldering pain tearing through him, his soul crying out for justice.

Kaplan must have been satisfied with what he read in Ford's eyes. "I'll send for Byron. He'll tell you what he saw."

Chapter Ten

When the enormity of Kaplan's statement burst like
fireworks in Denise's mind, excitement coursed
through her. Byron had *seen* something. Could he
give them a description of the Black Rose?

"Come," Kaplan gestured. "While you wait for
my son, I will show you my black roses."

"They are in bloom?" Ford asked.

"Come. You shall see."

Kaplan opened an umbrella and they followed him
into the rain and onto a partially closed-in rooftop. A
Zen garden with smooth, circular stones formed a
path past a tinkling waterfall that splashed into a granite basin set among the rocks. Bonsai, lit by in-ground
lights, had their own niche in the garden.

In spite of her excitement, a sense of wonder stole
over her. The balance of Eastern nature with its exquisite beauty set on a London rooftop subdued a
measure of her impatience.

Kaplan ambled, his head high, along a winding
path that took them toward several sprawling plants
and a greenhouse. Sensing he wouldn't be hurried,
she forced herself to match his snail's pace.

Finally, after she felt as if she'd been holding her breath for minutes, the Englishman closed his umbrella, entered the greenhouse and took them to a rear corner. "The Black Rose."

Denise edged through hot, cloying air and pressed her lips together tightly to avoid disclosing her disappointment. Sparse shrubs held three withered black blooms to each shriveled branch, each flower in the shape of a ragged open cup. A mere five to seven petals surrounded gray button centers as devoid of life as ashes. The scraggly plants didn't even have thorns.

She'd pictured long-stemmed graceful roses like the kind lovers sent on Valentine's Day—except, instead of deep crimson, the petals would be a pearl black. Although she knew there were thousands of varieties of roses, she would never have identified Kaplan's sickly-looking plants as roses if she hadn't been told otherwise. And she doubted the Swiss maid would have attributed this variety to the rose family, either.

Had they reached yet another dead end? She glanced anxiously at Ford. He arched an eyebrow and shrugged before turning back to their host.

"Ugly, aren't they?" Kaplan's lips turned up into a small smile. "You need not fear insulting me. I covet the ugliness amongst the beauty of the rest of the garden."

Denise guided the conversation back to a more concrete topic. "Have you ever sold these flowers?"

Kaplan chuckled. "Who would want to buy them?"

He had a point. Still, she hadn't flown halfway

around the world not to ask questions. "Can these flowers bloom at another time of year?"

"The black rose is very sensitive and it would not be easy. It might be possible. I have never tried."

"Have any ever been stolen?"

"No."

"Are Yvonne Jansen's black roses the same variety as yours?" Ford asked, though he knew the answer.

Kaplan led them to a delicate lattice structure inside the greenhouse where he gestured for them to sit. "I have never seen Mrs. Jansen's black roses and there are no pictures."

Surprised and curious at his last reply, Denise took a seat beside Ford. Anticipation had pumped her with an excess of adrenaline and energy. "Do you doubt the roses exist?"

Kaplan shook his head, surprising her again. Beside her, Ford tensed as the older man spoke, "Long ago, before the war, I saw a long-stemmed black rose with the most aromatic scent. Mr. Jansen had displayed the flower in France. All the newspaper boys took pictures, but the black rose never made it to print. Byron has searched."

So, Yvonne Jansen, the young rose breeder they'd met in Amsterdam, had married a man many years her senior. Or else Kaplan's Mr. Jansen was Yvonne's father-in-law. Denise supposed it didn't matter. At the rate they were finding clues, she'd be old and gray, or dead, before they figured out the assassin's identity.

Denise shifted, impatient to speak with Byron. "Do you know of anyone else who breeds black roses?"

Kaplan shook his head. At the sound of a footstep,

he rose to his feet and waited for his son to join them. Byron was taller and broader than his father, yet the similarities of a straight nose, thin lips and gaunt cheekbones remained.

She tried to keep the hope from her tone. "Your father mentioned you have seen the assassin we call the Black Rose."

"I was in a crowd at an embassy party in London five years ago," Byron said. "I saw only his back. He was as tall as me, about five foot ten, but thin. He was dressed in black and his short hair was also black, possibly a wig."

"How do you know the man you saw was the Black Rose?" Ford asked.

"I didn't know at the time. I put the facts together later. At the embassy, I heard the shots, saw the Italian ambassador stagger. The man in front of me dropped a gun to the floor and took off through the crowd."

"Was the assassin French?"

Byron shrugged. "The party was filled with Europeans, Canadians and Americans."

"The police couldn't trace the gun?" Denise guessed, already knowing the answer.

"That's correct. Later, I heard rumors of a black rose being found on the ambassador's pillow earlier that morning. During my travels, I've listened and read, but I've never found another clue."

Denise shivered and Ford put his arm around her. "And the black rose," Ford said. "Have you ever seen another besides your father's?"

"No. I'm sorry I don't have more to tell you. You have come a long way for nothing."

Her frustration mounted until she could barely sit still. "Is there anything else you can tell us?"

He hesitated, clearly reluctant to say more.

"Anything at all?" she pressed.

"I do not like to mention this because I am not sure. Remember, I was standing in a crowd. Many people surrounded me and I could easily have been mistaken. But I thought the Black Rose spoke in French before he fired."

Ford squeezed her hand. "Parisian French?"

"I don't know. I'm not even sure it was he who spoke the words."

"Can you remember what was said?"

"I'm sorry. I didn't speak the language very well then." He shrugged. "Perhaps if I heard it now..."

"What about the voice?" Denise asked.

Byron looked at her as if she were nuttier than a Snickers bar, yet he kept his demeanor polite. "What about the voice?"

"Was it high or low? Hurried or slow? Excited, happy, anxious?"

"Carefully articulated, yet whispery, as if he didn't wish to draw attention to himself."

Byron had told them all he could remember. After they exchanged phone, fax and E-mail numbers, promising to share any future information, they said goodbye and thanked their host.

Denise climbed into the back seat of another taxi with Ford, so jittery she felt ready to climb out of her skin. Before Ford gave the driver directions, she tapped his knee. "I don't know about you, but I'm not ready to sit on another airplane just yet."

Ford put an arm around her and gently tugged her against his side. "That was a waste of time."

"No clue, however minor, is a waste of time." She tried to remain professional and hide her disappointment when she'd also hoped to learn so much more.

His touch skidded electricity through her and she attributed the sensation to scrambled nerves. While he gave the driver directions to a hotel, she tried to regain her composure.

"It's unlikely Kaplan or his son have anything to do with the assassin." Ford rubbed his forehead. "Yvonne is too young to be the Black Rose, and her husband, who would be old enough, is dead. The assassin was around five foot ten—if he didn't add to his height with lifts in his shoes. He was thin five years ago when the Italian ambassador was assassinated, but he could be obese by now. And he may or may not speak French or have black hair."

She sighed at his unemotional summation. "We might not have a great description, but we learned the assassin is neither short nor tall. The assassin can blend into a crowd at an embassy party, which means he's acquired adequate social skills. Perhaps someone kept a party guest list?"

"I'll hire investigators and have them search police files of the assassination. Who knows, maybe we can uncover an old guest list."

She leaned her head back on his arm and looked up at him. How could he appear so patient while she was seething with disappointment and frustration? Then the car passed a lit billboard, and the impressive multicolored brilliance illuminated his sharply chiseled cheeks. He looked superbly handsome, all slash-ing angles and deeply tanned skin.

She trailed her fingers along his thigh. "You think we'll find more than Interpol did?"

"Old facts may seem insignificant until added to our new information." His mouth dipped closer to hers and although his words had sounded quite busi-nesslike, the smoothness of his tone was heated honey.

Her breath caught. "For instance?"

"It's a puzzle as difficult as reading a woman's mind."

Her heart hammered. He'd switched the conversa-tion to a much more personal level. Suddenly she re-alized all her mounting frustration, agitation and anx-iety were caused more by her growing feelings for Ford than her frustration over the slow pace of their investigation.

She closed her eyes in one last attempt to regain her senses. It annoyed her that she wanted him to touch her and that she wanted to touch him. Uncon-trollable heat shouldn't be spiraling through her. She wanted him, damned if she didn't. And she wanted him in every way.

Once again, he seemed to anticipate her emotions. He brushed her shoulder with his fingers, his touch as light as gossamer. Winding his fingers into her hair, he pulled her closer until she pressed against his rigid muscles. "Unless you share my room tonight, we'll fly home right away. The decision is yours, so tell me now—while I can still stop."

To think he had so little control over himself be-cause he wanted her shimmered excitement through her. She didn't say a word but lifted her lips to nibble his. Deliberately, she rubbed her breasts against him, teasing him, taunting him, knowing there could be no going back. Not wanting to go back.

She wanted Ford, and after all her vows to hold out for love and commitment, in this moment, her former qualms no longer mattered. Flattening herself against him seemed the most natural movement as she explored him with her fingers and mouth and tongue. Tonight he tasted of coffee and mint. He wore no cologne and his masculine fragrance combined with a sandalwood-scented soap enticed her to remain in his arms.

She exited the car and entered the London hotel in a dreamy haze, expecting to rip their clothes off and make mad, passionate love when they reached their room. But when Ford opened a door, she blinked. He hadn't taken her to a hotel room. Steam curled from a huge vacant whirlpool surrounded by a variety of lush tropical plants. The scent of incense hung heavy in the humid heat. Soft ground lights filtered upward, casting intimate shadows across the room. Dazed, she looked at him with confusion.

"I'll bathe you." He murmured suggestive, delicious words against her lips in a rough-soft tone.

"But—"

He grinned at her. "I've waited too long for this moment not to make it last."

Bending, he scooped her into his arms and lifted her. She flung her arms around his neck to maintain her balance. Flustered, still reeling from his kisses, she looked around the vacant room. "Suppose someone else comes in?"

"We won't be disturbed. And we weren't followed, I watched. But you can lock the door if you wish."

She freed one hand from around his neck, latched the door and turned back to him, feeling safe, secure and pampered, her stomach contorting in unfamiliar coils. "Now, where were we?"

"In the process of removing your clothes."

Embarrassed and breathless, she gulped as he carried her to a bench. "Mmm, Ford, there's something you should know."

"What?" he asked with a tender smile.

"I'm not very experienced."

His stride didn't falter. "It doesn't matter."

"You don't understand. I've never done this—"

"In a whirlpool?" He chuckled, his hand caressing her hip in sensual circles. "Neither have I. But I thought we should use a bed for our first time. I've reserved a private room off this one."

She drew a deep breath and forced the words past her lips. "I've never made love before. Period."

He didn't miss a step, but looked down at her, the fires in his eyes flaring so hot he made her feel like the most desirable woman in the world. Cocking one speculative eyebrow, he smiled. "Really?"

He obviously didn't know what to say. She'd probably shocked him. She supposed there were few twenty-nine-year-old virgins around. In one way, she wished for sophisticated experience to impress him. In another, she was glad she'd waited. He would be her first lover. She was his; she'd always been his.

His gaze focused on her mouth, increasing the quicksilver shiver in her stomach. She licked her top lip. "I should have told you before. I just never thought—"

"You can think...later."

Grateful he didn't ask questions about her past while her mind was in shambles, she reveled in the gentle touch of his hand that cupped her chin and skimmed her neck while they kissed. As she molded against him, seeking the closeness she'd fought so long, her breasts swelled. She'd never known she could be so sensitive there. Her nipples hardened, and for the first time in her life, she yearned for a man to touch her breasts.

Ford had other ideas. He seemed content to hold her on his lap and kiss her while his hands roamed over her back and bottom and thighs. Dizzily, she sought to control the newly awakened desire surging through her, but she couldn't stop the flow of passion. Either she wanted Ford too badly, or she was too new at making love to rein in her riotous feelings.

Finally, he broke the kiss to plant a trail of nips along her neck. "Slip the jacket from my shoulders." He issued instructions between delicious nibbles that had her shaking as she did as he asked.

With eager hands, she opened his shirt, the tips of her fingers grazing his chest and playing with the fine triangle of hairs that disappeared into the waistband of his pants. While removing his shirt, she smoothed her palms along his chest, lightly exploring his nipples in the process.

He sucked in his breath.

Enjoying the power she held over him, she teased him a bit more. This was her chance to caress his sculpted chest, trail her fingers over the ridges of muscles and delve to his rock-hard stomach, run her hands leisurely across him while he sighed in blissful appreciation.

She discovered he was ticklish.

And impatient. The wild pulse at his neck told her so. Yet he sat still, letting her do as she wished, watching her with an intensity that set her quivering.

When she sensed he wouldn't remain motionless for another second, she scooted off his lap and stood. He rose to his feet, and she unsnapped and unzipped his pants, the sounds loud in the hushed room. He kicked off his shoes and socks, stepped out of his slacks. As if sensing her hesitation to remove his boxer shorts, he took her back into his arms.

But she wouldn't turn coward now. Wriggling loose, she looped her thumbs into the waistband and tugged the garment down until it fell to the floor. He drew her tightly to him, and while he kissed her, she let her hand rove, marveling at his heat and learning him by touch. And there was a lot of him to learn.

"My turn," he whispered in her ear, sending a shiver of anticipation straight to her toes.

But he didn't remove her clothes, just stared into her eyes. She moistened dry lips. "Do you require my help?"

He breathed softly, and languidly met her gaze in an audacious yet sensual way. "Just stand still."

"Don't count on it."

When he walked behind her and unzipped her dress, her knees weakened. He grazed her skin with his fingertips, parted the material at her shoulders and eased her arms from her sleeves and then down past her hips while she held her breath. The dress rustled, and he moved slowly, teasing her in ways that felt both naughty and very, very nice.

He peeled her underwear off without touching her breasts. She remained standing, conscious of her nakedness, suffering momentary shyness and waiting for his touch to reassure her. At the sound of water splashing, she looked over her shoulder. He lifted a soapy cloth from a bucket and drizzled the warm sudsy water over her breasts.

"A whirlpool bath requires a wash before stepping into the tub," he told her with a husky tone.

Obviously his idea of a bath and hers were two different things. Her fingers trembled as it occurred to her that he intended to go much slower than she wanted.

She hurried him along by turning completely around. "I'm not going to make it to the bath."

Ignoring her words, he dropped his gaze from her eyes to her lips to her breasts. When he grinned like a starving man eyeing a feast, she'd never been more grateful for her overabundance. He swirled the cloth along her collarbone, the water raining down in fiery rivulets, and she squirmed under his lightest touch.

Arching her back, she reached for him. "I've waited long enough," she gasped. "Don't make me wait anymore."

"Let me rinse off the soap, so I can dry you."

He lifted a bucket over her head, and she raised her face to the water, and arched her back, hoping the clear rinse water would cool her hot flesh. The fever he'd created, the one only he could cure, burned her.

Being one with him consumed her. She used every ounce of willpower to refrain from tackling him to the wooden decking and demanding he make love with her.

Finally, he took her hand and led her to a door she hadn't noticed before.

"Wait, I need a towel."

He grinned. "What for?"

"You said you'd dry me."

"And I fully intend to keep that promise. I'll dry you with my tongue."

They never made it to the bed but eased onto a thick terry towel just inside the door. He made good on his promise, licking the water from her flesh and creating such provocative sensations she gasped in sheer mindless pleasure.

When his lips closed over first one nipple and then the other, shock waves surged through every aching nerve. She moaned, soft little erotic noises. He found the curves of her breasts and gently fondled her until she writhed, frenzied and out of control.

"Please," she begged barely recognizing her voice, so redolent of pleasure.

"Please what?"

"Now. I want you inside me, now."

He claimed her mouth while he parted her thighs. His fingers slipped between her curls and found her slick, warm and ready. Frantic with wanting him, she arched her back to meet him.

Ignoring her demand, he continued an extended, carnal exploration with his fingers that left her gasping and crying out hoarse whimpers of bliss. Unbearable need had her clutching his shoulders, his hips, demanding an end to the searing desire.

"Easy," he said in a low, husky voice. "I don't want to hurt you."

"Going easy is killing me. Do it."

When he hesitated, she seized his hips and arched to meet him. She felt no pain, only scintillating pressure as he filled her, stretching her.

His eyes smoldered and the pulsing muscle in his jaw revealed his effort to hold back. "Are you okay?"

"I'm tingling all over. I didn't know you would feel so good."

"Patience. The best is yet to come."

He moved slowly, letting her become accustomed to him. She quickly learned that she liked best the long sensual strokes that quickened in tune to the beat pulsing inside her.

With her head thrown back and her eyes closed, she felt wanton, wonderful, pure woman. He caressed her breasts, his fingers plucking at her nipples, taking her over the edge. She gasped his name. He kissed her again. A moment later, his body shuddered with release.

Afterward, he held her gently, his hands smoothing the hair from her face. "Next time, we'll go slower," he promised.

The idea of a next time pleased her. Her life changing so incredibly in just a few short hours was wonderful and frightening. Yet, Ford hadn't promised her a thing. He hadn't indicated his feelings. He might consider their lovemaking no more than a pleasant interlude. So while she'd given him her body, at least she could keep her pride, and she bit back words of

love. Instead, she gave in to the fiery sensations over-
taking her once more.

As his tongue swirled over her breasts with the del-
icacy of baby's breath, she lost herself in pure sensation. He made love to her so many times she lost
count. Eventually they returned to the whirlpool and
soaked. While they didn't sleep that night, she regretted waiting so long, sensing their time together
whirring to a resolution. Tomorrow they would fly
back to the States. Tomorrow, she would begin to lose
him.

Chapter Eleven

After their plane landed in New Orleans, Ford held
Denise back when she started to stand. "Let the other
passengers deplane first."

"Why?"

"I've arranged round-the-clock protection. I'd like
to take you to my home or my parents' home, but
we'd be too easy to find. Until the Black Rose is
caught, I'm not risking your life."

But it's my life.

While she couldn't fault him for protecting them,
and felt good that he still wanted her with him, she
was miffed that once again he'd forgotten to discuss
the arrangements. But she was too travel-weary to
protest. She'd been sitting for so long she'd swear her
body had permanently molded to the shape of the
seat.

In some ways, Ford appeared to be the same man
who'd made love to her, at first tenderly, then furiously, and again gently. Until he'd held her in his
arms, she hadn't known what it felt like to be cherished, wanted, needed. And it felt damn good.

Yet, in other ways, he was very different today.

Today he broadcast focused intensity. Once his world enveloped him, she lost him. Sharing his life when he didn't slow down long enough between phone calls for her to ask questions seemed impossible. On the plane, he'd eaten dinner as he negotiated for the holographic imaging company in Silicon Valley. While she read a magazine, he'd sent a prime breeding stallion from his Ocala horse farm to Jacques in France. Even she knew a former Kentucky Derby winner had to be worth a fortune, and she admired his generous gesture. But still, she was annoyed that he hadn't consulted her about security arrangements.

Just then, two large men captured her attention as they entered the plane, their eyes darting in professional sweeps. Although Ford was tall, these men towered over him by several inches, and each man moved with the grace of an athlete, sporting honed muscles over big frames.

"Where did you find them?" she asked.

"They are all ex–Secret Service agents who work for Norton Industries."

The bodyguards escorted them off the plane to the tarmac and a waiting limousine. "Has the bullet-proof glass been installed in the office windows at Norton?" Ford asked after he settled her inside the limo.

"Yes, sir," said the team leader in the front seat, who'd introduced himself as the Doctor. "But the renovations to your home are not yet finished. Martin briefed us at headquarters this morning and said to bring you to his house. With the high walls around his property, we can protect you better there than at a hotel."

"Martin put you on the job this morning?"

"Yes, sir. About an hour ago. We just flew in from guarding an oil tanker in the gulf."

"How big is your team?"

"Four men and two dogs," the Doctor said.

"Are you rested and alert?"

"Yes, sir."

While Denise admired Ford's thoroughness, she wondered if he'd mind if she checked the backgrounds on these men once they arrived. Or had he already done so?

"How long has your team been together?"

"Five years."

"Good. If I like your work, you'll receive a bonus."

The Doctor didn't crack a smile. "Thank you, sir. We haven't yet checked out either house. It'll take a day or two for us to be up to speed."

"Not good enough. You have until tonight when Norton Industries hosts the annual stockholders' meeting."

As the limo pulled out of Moisant International, New Orleans' airport, onto Highway 10, heading toward City Park, Denise focused on Ford. Although she would have preferred that he'd discussed his action with her, she approved of his using bodyguards, it made her job easier. Now while the hired men watched entrances and exits, she'd only have to worry about protecting him.

The necessity of hiding behind bullet-proof glass was all her fault. If she hadn't kidnapped him, he wouldn't need bodyguards. Her heart skipped as she realized he'd be a prime target tonight. When he spoke, he'd be spotlighted on the stage of one of the largest hotels just outside the French Quarter. There was no surefire way to protect him, and with a company as successful as his, Norton must have thousands of stockholders.

The Doctor shook his head. "I suggest you cancel the speech."

"I agree." She took Ford's hand.

He shook his head. "There's too much riding on this meeting for me to avoid an appearance. However, I've made preparations, a glare-proof, bullet-proof glass screen will shield the stage. The manufacturer assures me the screen won't be detected by the audience."

"How tall is the screen?" the bodyguard asked.

"Twenty feet. That should cover anyone with a rifle in the balcony."

The Doctor whistled. "You don't believe in doing things halfway."

"What happens if the Black Rose discharges a weapon at the glass?" Denise asked. "Could a ricocheting bullet injure the audience?"

Ford squeezed her hand. "No chance of that. The glass absorbs almost all the projectile's momentum." He spoke again to the Doctor. "Martin has a layout of the building we rented for the evening. Hire extra men if you need them, but no one you haven't known for at least two years. I don't want a surprise coming at our backs."

As they drove from the airport, Ford briefed the Doctor on the Black Rose. Denise saved her energy and contributed nothing more to the conversation. She marveled at Ford's vigor. He'd made love all night and written his speech between phone calls on the way back. Tonight he would host his most important meeting of the year.

If he'd slept, she hadn't caught him with his eyes closed. She wouldn't be surprised if he dropped with exhaustion, but he looked as energetic and rested as if he'd just spent a week lolling on the beach.

Ford had taken care of everything, which left her nothing to do but worry. Her neck prickled, and she looked around warily.

MARTIN'S HOME was surrounded by a brick wall and a guarded gate, seemingly safe enough. The driver stopped, rolled down the electric window a mere inch and conferred with a third guard. While she breathed in a whiff of balmy air, she memorized the guard's plain-faced features, wondering why her sixth sense had kicked in when she saw nothing to arouse her suspicion.

The three-story house with columns, gallery and a wing on each end had been beautifully restored. Massive live oaks shaded empty and immaculate lawns. There were no sudden shadows or movements behind the windows. The conversation around her was normal. Yet, the scent of danger strangled the air.

"Grounds are secure, sir," the guard reported.

The Doctor leaned toward the window. "Any problems?"

"None out here. We haven't been inside yet."

The Doctor shut his window. "You folks stay in the car until I check out the house."

While the driver and the Doctor entered the house, Denise fidgeted in her seat and turned to Ford. "Surely we're safe in the yard. Your man just said so. I'd like to stretch my legs a bit.'' And she wanted a look around. All this security was great, but she needed to allay her misgivings. She'd never forgive herself if she ignored her instincts and failed to protect the man she loved.

Ford accompanied her as she exited the car. ''I'm sorry if I've ignored you. I hadn't planned to be out of touch so long, and there were lots of details to clear up.''

The limo phone rang. They walked back to the car, Ford answered and she waited impatiently until he hung up.

''That was the bank investigator I hired. He traced the payment to the assassin to Amsterdam. The money is still there.''

Denise's hopes rocketed. ''Has the money been withdrawn?''

''Not one penny was touched.''

''Did he get a name?''

''He should have one within the hour.'' The phone rang again and Ford picked it up. ''Hi, Max.''

She wandered away and gave him the privacy to speak with his brother. Ford kept the call short and joined her within minutes. ''My life isn't always this hectic.''

''Really?''

''Hey.'' He stopped walking and cupped her chin. ''Give me a few days and then I'll slow down enough to explain, okay? Right now, I have to concentrate on protecting us.''

''That's my job,'' she insisted.

A startled glimmer lit his blue eyes. ''Bear with me?''

He won points for not arguing, and for an answer, she kissed him. When he released her, she was breathless, the tension between them diminished.

She turned toward Martin's grand, three-story house decorated with coupled columns, monumental steps, wall surfaces with pilasters and a sculpted classical figure by a fountain. It had a chilly feel to it, lacking a woman's touch, and she recalled Martin was a bachelor.

Hand in hand they strolled toward the front steps where the driver waited for them. "We found a cook, a maid and Martin's gardener living over the garage. The Doc is clearing the upstairs areas before you enter."

A slender, gray-haired man dressed in a suit and tie exited the house. His thin face was almost hidden by thick black-framed glasses, a mustache and neat goatee.

"Is that Martin?" she whispered as the brown-eyed man approached.

Ford shook his head and frowned. "I don't recognize him, but he seems familiar."

The driver checked his clipboard. "He's the cook. He'll return to prepare the evening meal at around five o'clock."

Ford shrugged. "I suppose I've met him at one of Martin's dinners."

Without saying a word, the cook tipped his hat and walked by. They continued to wait outside while the Doctor took a long time to inspect the house. Finally, the head security agent came outside.

The moment Denise saw his steely eyes, her instincts kicked into life. "What's wrong?"

"The house is safe, but you should see what I found."

They climbed a wide flight of stairs, strode over Persian carpets and down a hall of gilded mirrors and Renaissance art. The Doctor motioned them to enter a white bedroom at the back of the house. An alabaster chintz spread covered the canopy bed. Two lacy pillows lay at the headboard.

On each pillow lay a single black rose.

Her heart slammed her ribs. On rubbery legs, she shuffled toward the bed. The rose had a long stem with half-inch thorns. The bloom was coal-black with petals that curled in at the tips.

"Don't touch anything," Ford said.

Every nerve in her body signaled danger, but she couldn't resist a quip. "I just want to smell the roses."

"Very funny."

She bent toward the flower and inhaled. The overpowering scent sickened her. "These have the aromatic scent Kaplan described. If we take a picture and fax it, he can tell us if this variety is the same as the London black rose."

"Damn! Stop the cook!" Ford spun on his heel, sprinted pell-mell down the hall, leaped three steps at a time and charged out the front door.

Startled by his actions, she and the Doctor raced after him. They didn't catch Ford until he'd stopped at the front gate.

"Sir?" the Doctor asked.

The hairs on her nape lifted and goose bumps angled down her back. "Ford, what is it?"

"I know why the cook looked familiar." Ford pounded his fist into his palm.

"The cook?" The Doctor peered through the gate down the empty road. "What about him?"

"The gray-haired man who passed us as we came in?" Denise asked with a frown.

At Ford's hint, she realized the cook's brown eyes had seemed familiar to her, too, but she'd discounted the possibility of knowing anyone in this fancy neighborhood.

Ford sprinted back to the house. "Only the *he* is a *she*."

"Yvonne Jansen?" she guessed aloud as she ran at his side. "But she's too young to have committed all the assassinations."

"Maybe she's a copycat. But it makes sense. The black roses on our pillows. Her showing up here. The bank money in Amsterdam. Why didn't she kill us when we visited her home?"

"We took her by surprise. And she's a pro who wouldn't panic and make a hit without careful preparation. She wouldn't risk dead bodies in her home and a police investigation."

In the foyer, Ford grabbed the phone, dialed and said into the receiver, "Anne, I need that information on Yvonne Jansen, her family, her dead husband, her business, if she has a criminal record."

The Doctor entered the hallway. "We're moving you from here. The police put out an APB and we'll notify Interpol."

"Don't bother." Denise sank into a chair. "That woman has a hundred disguises. With her ten-minute head start, the police won't find her. And if we leave, she'll no doubt follow. With your security team now in place and the high walls around the house, we're safer here than at a hotel. How did she gain access?''

The Doctor checked his list. "She gave us the real cook's name, and I've just learned this is his day off. I'm sorry. This would never have happened if we'd been on the job more than a few hours.''

Denise fought to keep her voice even. "The black roses indicate she's making her hit tonight.''

Ford dropped the receiver into its cradle. "Damn. She couldn't have picked a worse night.''

"You can't go on that stage," Denise said with a sinking feeling he wouldn't listen.

He raked a hand through his hair and his eyes hardened. "You don't understand. The only way to catch the assassin is with bait.''

And he intended to be the bait. Horror rose to choke her. "No!''

"It's the only way. Only you and I can recognize Yvonne. We don't have her picture. Anne thought the woman was simply camera shy. Now we know why. But if the Black Rose is coming tonight, it's our chance to nab her.''

FORD, DENISE AND the Doctor spent the rest of the day preparing for the stockholders' meeting. The posh New Orleans hotel had one of the most convenient locations in town—directly on the Mississippi River on the Canal Street edge of the French Quarter. The window-walled tenth-floor lobby was a masterpiece of Carrara marble, fine paintings and antiques. The rooms boasted marble foyers and baths, antique furnishings and plush king-size beds. Ignoring the weeping river and French Quarter views that were truly spectacular, Denise was more concerned with security.

As she, Ford and the Doctor walked with his security team through the hotel's ground floor where the meeting would be held this evening, Ford's phone rang. The team spread out in all directions while Ford listened for several minutes, then put down the phone.

"That was a senator who owes me a favor and has a connection in Interpol. Yvonne's husband was killed by a bullet between the eyes. He also grew black roses. It is believed that after Yvonne's husband was killed, she inherited both businesses."

"She took on his assassination work?" Denise frowned. "The pieces fit. Her husband must have done the earlier killings."

"Yvonne's fluent in French, and her husband was thirty-nine years older."

Yvonne's husband was old enough to have been a young man displaying roses in London after World War II. Denise remembered Yvonne had called the black roses *la fleur du mort,* the death flower—a fitting name for an assassin—and in French.

As Ford continued to make phone calls, an apprehensive chill shimmied down her spine. If Yvonne had been paid in full by Henschel, why was she still after Ford when Henschel was dead?

Had the assassin feared she and Ford would succeed in exposing the Black Rose's identity? Had their investigation forced Yvonne to come after them? No. Yvonne had known they were on her trail *before* she and Ford contacted Grendal. While a leak at the British embassy could explain Yvonne's picking up their intentions so quickly, there were several other possibilities. Perhaps Yvonne kept tabs on Ford's private jet. Or there was a security leak. Something didn't fit and the ambiguities bothered her. They still didn't have all the puzzle pieces.

Oblivious to her worries, Ford suddenly covered the phone's mouthpiece. "What do you want to wear tonight?"

She appreciated his remembering to ask her. There might be hope for his high-handed tendencies yet. Putting aside her premonition of disaster, she held out her hand for the phone and spoke directly to Anne. "Would a pantsuit be appropriate?"

"Yes," the secretary said.

"Okay, then I'd appreciate your finding one that's loose enough to wear a bullet-proof vest underneath. And Ford should wear one, too. I want sneakers on my feet—no heels."

Ford cocked his eyebrow as he listened. At her last request, he shook his head.

"I may have to run. Also, I'll need a shoulder-strap purse large enough to hold a handgun. That's it. Thanks, Anne."

Ford switched off the phone, and as they entered the empty but ornate auditorium that would be filled to capacity tonight, he took her into his arms. He looked grim. "I'm letting you come with me only because if I didn't, you'd come alone."

"I've met Yvonne. With both of us looking, we stand a better chance of spotting her."

He ran his hands up and down her arms and stared straight into her eyes. "I'd pay one of Doc's men to keep you someplace safe, except I don't think you'd forgive me.''

"I wouldn't." While she relished his concern and was warmed by his protectiveness, she stood firm. No way was she sitting at home worrying while he took all the risks. "The Doctor assured me he can disguise me so my own mother won't recognize me. I'll be safe."

His expression didn't change. Clearly, her words hadn't satisfied him. "Once we spot the Black Rose, promise me you'll let the Doctor and his team handle her."

"I have no intention of confronting Yvonne," she assured him truthfully.

She was about to make him promise to do the same, when a short, balding man with a paunch approached, his shiny shoes squeaking on the plush maroon carpet. An unlit cigar hung from the corner of his mouth. "It's about time you got back."

Ford shook the man's hand. "Denise, I'd like you to meet Martin Crewsdale, my partner."

Denise offered her hand, and Martin pumped it enthusiastically. He winked at her, removed the cigar and pointed it toward her. "So you're the reason he's late. But I'm sure Ford will pull off the stockholders' meeting with élan, he always does."

When Ford started to fill in Martin on the security arrangements and the surprise presentation on the holographic equipment he'd flown in from Silicon Valley at the last moment, Martin put up his hand like a cop stopping traffic. "I don't need details. I've got problems of my own."

"What problems?" Ford asked.

"I haven't learned who's buying Norton stock," Martin complained. "The buyer is smart. They're moving slowly but steadily, managing not to run up the price."

"What percentage?"

"As of this morning, twenty-five percent. The entire operation has your handwriting on it. You sure you know nothing about it?"

Ford's eyes narrowed. "My capital is tied up in the Silicon deal. Besides, if I intended to buy more stock, I'd have told you."

Martin puffed on his cigar and blew a ring of smoke. "Sorry. I heard a rumor with your name attached."

"You heard wrong. What else have you got?"

Martin started a detailed explanation of bylaws, voting rights and amendments. Ford had been correct about his partner's tendency to worry over every detail.

More interested in the security arrangements than the men's discussion, Denise wandered down the gently sloping floor toward the stage. One of the Doctor's men remained with Ford while another agent shadowed her.

Ford had explained how the firm needed to balance looking prosperous with appearing careful of stockholders' money. She strolled between the dinner tables set with crisp linen, gleaming silver and fine china, thinking his company had done a good job. Frilly white carnations surrounded delicate lavender orchids at the center of each table, looking elegant but not extravagant.

The bullet-proof glass shield that would protect the

elevated stage had not yet arrived. Ford had explained that the Doctor's team would make certain that the entire area was vacant before the glass would be set in place on the stage and a cordoned-off area would keep guests away. Timing was critical. The glass had to be in place just moments before the guests arrived to prevent the Black Rose from discovering their deception with a last-minute walk-through.

Denise ambled across the stage and sat, letting her legs dangle and swing over the edge. If she were the assassin, from where would she take her shot? From among the guests at the nearby tables? From the seats that rose in steps along the sides and back of the room?

Tilting her chin, she stared upward. Metal I beams crisscrossed the ceiling. Lights dangled from steel supports. A small room, up high, by the ceiling, would ensure a perfect shot at the stage. She imagined that lighting and sound people worked in the small, elevated booth during theater productions. In addition to the itch on the back of her neck, a bad feeling clutched her stomach as she stared at the darkened room. She'd mention to the Doctor that one of his men should stand guard there. Not that she needed to be telling ex–Secret Service agents how to do their jobs—but still, it never hurt to be thorough.

Ford would also be vulnerable from behind. But six burly guards would prevent anyone from going backstage.

The Doctor had every corner of the room and each entrance and exit staked out. So why was her stomach tied into one big pretzel? And why was the back of her neck prickling?

ALTHOUGH DENISE LOOKED very different in makeup, and should be unrecognizable to the assassin, she shuddered to think what Ford would say if he discovered her deception. However, she couldn't let his feelings interfere with her work. She'd been hired to find the assassin and that's what she intended to do. Besides, she and Ford would never be safe until Yvonne was behind bars.

Denise now had a wider nose, fuller lips and darker skin. The bullet-proof vest disguised her curves and a chestnut wig hid her golden-blond curls.

When Ford had told her that he usually greeted the stockholders as they entered the hotel auditorium, she'd asked him and the board members to remain backstage. The Doctor had agreed. Hopefully no one could pass through the cordoned-off area, and the protective glass was now in place. As long as Ford remained onstage, he'd be safe.

Ford probably assumed she would remain with him. However, when he'd turned to greet a business associate, she'd slipped away to change clothes and apply the makeup and wig. She'd never intended to remain backstage but hadn't discussed her plan with Ford, then lied to the doctor, saying Ford had approved her scheme.

The Doctor took Denise's arm, and they wandered through the increasingly crowded room. Knowing Yvonne might disguise herself as a male or a female, Denise carefully searched every face. If she spotted the Black Rose before Yvonne disrupted the meeting, and the Doctor's men apprehended the assassin, Denise could stop worrying about Ford's safety.

The Doctor suggested they ignore anyone over six

foot or under five foot three inches in height, but the majority of people fell between those parameters. The Doctor leaned down toward Denise. "Anything?"

"Zip. How long does the cocktail party last?"

"Forty-five minutes. We only have ten left."

When the crowd took their seats, it would be easier to ensure she didn't miss a face in the crowd. But the room was enormous, and after the stockholders settled at their tables, she wouldn't have the freedom of movement she had now.

She needed to find Yvonne soon. Despite the guards and the protective glass, Denise couldn't curb the feeling they'd overlooked something.

Craning her head, she looked upward and yanked on the Doctor's arm. "Didn't you post a guard in the lighting booth upstairs? I don't see him."

The Doctor peered up and frowned. "I don't see David, either."

The Doctor reached into his pocket, signaled, and within moments one of his men joined them.

"Have you seen Yvonne?" the agent asked.

"No, and David's not in sight."

The agent spoke quietly into his microphone. "There's no answer. I'll check on him."

"I'll go with you," the Doctor said.

Denise accompanied the two men, hoping the Doctor wouldn't forbid her presence. She looped an arm through his, making it more difficult for him to slip away. "If there aren't any problems, maybe I can spot Yvonne from up there."

The Doctor shook his head. "You'll be too far away to see individual faces. Besides, Ford wouldn't want you in danger. Stay here and I'll assign another of my men to you.''

"No need to take a man off the job. Besides, I brought binoculars,'' she argued, strolling toward an exit, paying no mind to his suggestion to stay in the crowd. "But I won't endanger myself or get in your way. I'll wait until you give me the go-ahead.'' She sensed him weakening. "Come on, I'm the only one who can positively identify her. Besides, the hairs on my neck are standing straight up.''

"What does that mean?'' the Doctor asked as he held her back and let the other agent go ahead of them.

"My instincts are kicking in. She's upstairs. I feel it.''

They climbed the steps, following the agent but at a distance. With a team member already upstairs, the Doctor apparently wasn't too concerned about allowing her to accompany him.

"Can you see the guy who is supposed to be here?'' Denise whispered as they climbed a narrow flight of stairs.

"No. Stay here.''

The Doctor pursued the guard into the booth. The door shut behind the agents. What the hell was going on? The men disappeared into the lighting booth but no one came out. Why hadn't the Doctor signaled her?

Uneasy, Denise looked ahead. She held her breath. Heard nothing. Saw nothing.

Unwilling to make a sound and reveal her presence, she reached for her gun. Her heart raced. Ford would be furious if he found out she was up here. She should return to the auditorium. But suppose the Doctor needed help? Or didn't recognize Yvonne?

Denise would take only one peek. Ducking below the glass panel in the upper half of the door, she slowly and silently turned the knob. Pulled the door open.

Gripping the gun, she crouched, then walked through the opening, her gaze sweeping the dim booth with a glance. Empty. Except for the Doctor.

"You were supposed to wait downstairs," he hissed.

"You may need help," she insisted.

But this was one time her instincts were wrong. Still, she didn't breathe with relief until she spotted a second door on the far side on the booth. The guard they had followed up here must be scouting ahead. Perhaps David had just needed a bathroom break. The Doctor reached to switch on the lights.

Denise stopped him by tugging him to the front glass panel overlooking the stage. "I can see better in the dark," she whispered. Her voice trembled, and she ignored how much she disliked dark, enclosed spaces by focusing on Ford.

He was easy to pick out among his board of directors. For one thing, he towered over most of them. But even from up here, the confident way he moved was easily picked out in the crowd.

She raised the binoculars and saw one of the agents hand Ford the note she'd left which said, "Good luck. I'll be watching." She hoped the note would allay his suspicions about her whereabouts.

"Did you find David?" she murmured to the Doctor.

"Why are you whispering?"

"Something's wrong."

"What?" He spun, searching the booth.

"I'm not sure."

She glanced around the empty booth again. A desk stood in front of the window. There was nothing else in here, except a trash can in the corner, several magazines on the floor, a dirty ashtray and the dim lights from the stage switches.

Something creaked, sounding stealthy rather than careless. She heard a squeaky noise, but there was only carpeting under their feet.

A cold sweat trickled down her neck. Below, people took their seats. She should get the hell out of here before she was hurt—or worse. Let the Doctor's team deal with her suspicions. Yet, if there was one chance she could make a difference...

The Doctor motioned her back down the stairs. Heart pounding, she pretended not to see his gesture. Instead, she searched the tiny booth. Cool sweat slid clammily down her neck. Coming up here probably had been a mistake. If she hurried, she could remove the makeup and find Ford backstage.

But if she made the wrong decision and lost Ford to the Black Rose's bullet, she'd never forgive herself. Steeling her resolve, she inched into the darkest part of the booth toward a shadow that pricked her interest. Her searching fingers found a closet door set flush in the wall.

Taking a step backward, she motioned the Doctor to cover her and reached for the handle. Her heart leaped into her throat.

"Don't!" He clamped a hand on her shoulder and pulled her back to the steps.

Eerily, by its own accord, the door creaked open. A body tumbled out.

Chapter Twelve

David! Denise swallowed back a scream. She fought down bone-icing fear. With his head cocked at a peculiar angle, the burly man had to be dead.

The guard she and the Doctor had followed must have heard the commotion and stepped back into the dim booth, dismissing the area behind him with a wave of his hand. "This is a dead end."

The Doctor pointed his gun at the closet. "We've found David. But if the Black Rose isn't using this booth to shoot from, why did she kill him?"

The Black Rose was a professional. She didn't kill out of spite. She needed this booth. But then why wasn't she here? Where had she gone? Denise shivered, grateful for the bullet-proof vest that added warmth to her pantsuit, but then she forced herself forward.

She searched the closet for a hidden opening or secret passage. "There's nothing here. Let's search—"

"Shh." The agent put his finger to his lips. "I heard a noise in the ceiling."

Tilting back her head, she could just make out ceiling tiles in the dropped ceiling. Was the Black Rose above them?

The agent must have had the same thought. Striding to the desk, he climbed to look and flipped on the light switch. A blue light zigzagged over the agent's arm. With a stammering shriek, the agent collapsed to the floor and the sickening odor of burnt flesh permeated the musty room.

The Doctor yanked her against the wall. "She booby-trapped the light switch."

"How? When?"

"Yesterday or the day before. No one got past our security today." The Doctor advanced and kneeled over the agent, checking his injuries. "She probably activated a timer. There's no way we could have spotted her trick without removing every electrical plate in the building."

Even Ford wouldn't expect them to have taken the walls apart.

The Doctor's voice filled with relief. "He's alive."

Below, the audience must be taking their seats. One of the board members blew softly into the microphone. The lights dimmed. And her flesh prickled from her neck all the way down her back.

The Doctor spoke into his microphone. "I need an ambulance ASAP. We've got two men down in the lighting booth."

A horrible suspicion that had niggled in the back of her mind burst to the forefront of her thoughts. Her stomach tightened. "Listen to me!" She pointed at the ceiling. "Maintenance must have access to change the ceiling lightbulbs. If an electrical access tunnel runs from this booth to behind the stage, Ford may be in danger.''

The Doctor swore, leaped onto the desk and shoved aside the overhead panel. "Go get help. I'm after—"

Denise rushed to the door. Since he could call for help on his microphone, she knew he was either sending her to safety or he didn't want to pull another agent off his assigned task. Before she'd taken two steps, the sickening thunk of a solid object hit flesh. The Doctor groaned and crashed.

She spun, watching, listening. The Doctor didn't move. When she heard the soft shuffle of someone crawling away, Denise approached and fumbled over his chest to his neck but couldn't find a pulse. Downstairs, the opening speaker welcomed the audience. Above, metal groaned as the assassin worked her way down the tunnel.

The Black Rose was crawling above the stage and behind the protective panel. Denise had to stop her before she took a shot at Ford. But how?

Ignoring the burning fear in her gut, the stabbing panic behind her eyes, the terror pounding at the base of her skull, she forced herself to think what to do. Beside her the Doctor moaned. He was alive, didn't appear shot or stabbed. But she had no idea how badly he was injured.

Blood roared in her ears. Should she get help? Or go after the Black Rose alone?

A snap decision was mandatory. Denise had only seconds to make the most important decision of her life. She considered the Black Rose's head start and concluded she'd never find help and return before the assassin reached her target.

Climbing onto the desk, Denise stuck her head through the hole. A tunnel led into blackness. A shudder racked her and she braced against overwhelming, mind-numbing horror. If she crawled into the vent and panicked, she couldn't turn around, couldn't retreat. But leaving Ford to die was intolerable, and she hung on to that thought with a slippery grasp. If only she could scream out and warn him.

The microphone.

She scrambled to the floor and felt the Doctor's neck for the wire that ran to his ear. Somehow in the fall, he'd torn the wire from the microphone. *Damn.* She turned to the burned agent. His headset had shorted out from the electrical shock.

Oh, God!

Don't panic.

Don't panic.

Don't panic!

Even as she estimated that the time down the stairs and across the auditorium would take too long, she edged to the black tunnel, forcing back terror. They'd planned for every contingency, protecting Ford's back—but they'd never expected the Black Rose to penetrate their tight ring of security and come in from behind the bullet-proof screen for her shot.

Below, on the stage, Martin stepped to the podium. Ford's turn would be soon. And if she let Ford die because she was afraid of the dark, she'd never forgive herself.

She turned the shoulder strap until her purse rested against her back. While she couldn't easily reach her gun, the arrangement left her hands free. Climbing onto the desk, she again peered into the tunnel. She couldn't see far. The metal angled upward, above the auditorium's ceiling and toward the stage. She broke into a sweat at the thought of crawling through pitch blackness.

Her wig itched, and she tossed it to the floor. Below, the speaker paused, the audience applauded, then the speaker picked up the pace.

Go.

She could breathe in the darkness but that didn't stop her from inhaling one deep breath before pulling herself into the dank, overhead crawl space. Leaving the open room and the murky light behind and dragging herself into blackness caused her palms to slicken with sweat.

Without enough room to crawl, she slithered on her belly, soldier style. As she advanced, the feeble dimness behind her disappeared. Her breath sounded too loud, and to calm herself, she concentrated on inhaling through her nose and exhaling through her mouth.

Ford's bullet-proof glass would be useless if Yvonne shot him in the back. Denise had to stop the Black Rose, overcome the terror that paralyzed forward movement. Her breathing came in sharp, jagged gasps. She had to go on. The tunnel should end somewhere behind the stage.

Move.

Knowing the assassin held every advantage alarmed her. No matter how quietly she crawled, the metal vibrated. And when she reached the end of the tunnel, Yvonne would be waiting.

There would be no place for Denise to hide.

SOON NOW, very soon, the long chase would be over. The plan would come together. The Black Rose would succeed. Ford Braddack and Denise Ward would finally be dead. And Norton Industries would be in new hands, better-qualified hands.

ONSTAGE FORD WONDERED where Denise had wandered off to. The note she'd left had been in her handwriting. Although he'd assumed she'd watch from backstage, at first he hadn't been too concerned with her disappearance. But with the speeches about to start, he'd asked one of the guards to find out if the Doctor had seen her.

Moments ago, the guard informed him that the Doctor wasn't responding to their calls. Neither were two other agents—one posted in the auditorium, the other upstairs in the lighting booth. The problem could be due to electronic interference, and the man assured him it was nothing to worry about. But an icy chill invaded Ford's soul.

Where was Denise? She should have remained backstage with him. He'd seen her slip off to the ladies' room but hadn't seen her come out. Could she be sick?

He asked a guard to check and waited impatiently for an answer. The guard told him the rest room was empty, and she must have taken a seat in the audience to watch his speech.

Just when Ford considered searching for her, Martin called the meeting to order.

AHEAD, DENISE SPIED a lighter grayness amid the inky black. The end of the tunnel! Tightening her grip on her weapon, she accelerated her pace.

Again she heard the audience applaud and feared Ford was walking to the podium. She forced her aching thighs to move faster and wriggled ahead.

The tunnel suddenly vibrated. Was someone behind her? She couldn't wait for reinforcements. As Ford spoke his opening remarks, his voice filtered up to her and made her hurry. Every word he uttered was a countdown to his death.

She pulled herself to the tunnel's end and looked out at ceiling panels too thin to hold her weight. The metal tubing ended over the middle of the stage. She could see through cracks that Ford and the board members had congregated along the stage's front and close to the audience. A curtain hung behind the board members and prevented the audience from seeing what happened on or above the stage.

Far below her, wagons filled with hay bales for a western musical that would appear next week littered the stage. Still, from this height, a fall would be fatal. So where had the Black Rose gone? Directly below and to either side of Denise were lights. Peering through the ceiling panels, she spied metal I beams.

Was the assassin waiting for her to emerge from the tunnel and onto the I beams before taking a shot? Or was it possible that Yvonne didn't know Denise had followed her through the tunnel and would be looking ahead toward her target, not back toward Denise?

From the position on her stomach, Denise couldn't see Yvonne. Yvonne couldn't see her. But as soon as she poked her head out to follow the assassin onto the I beams below, Denise would be an easy target.

Would Yvonne shoot her the moment she was exposed? Risky or not, she had to do something. Fast.

Denise glanced down again, this time ignoring the height and the danger. She searched for a place to lower herself where she could remain hidden from Yvonne.

There was none.

She spied a bright light shining forward from the back of the stage. If she kept the light at her back, Yvonne might be blinded by it. Hoping the assassin would focus forward on her target, Denise removed a ceiling panel. Praying the thin steel would hold her weight, Denise lowered herself to the beam.

Luckily, she had no abnormal fear of heights.

She lurched and grabbed a handhold. Where was Yvonne?

The curtains and the many I beams blocked a shot at Ford from here. Yvonne would have to move closer to him. Ahead, she spotted a figure in black clothing advancing across the I beams toward the podium, her heart tripped.

Yvonne!

Denise decided against calling out to Ford. If he heard her voice, he'd come running and make the assassin's job easier.

Keeping the bright light behind her, Denise skirted a vertical beam and inched along the slippery metal. She had to stop the assassin before the woman squeezed off a shot. While the crisscrossing beams protected Ford, the cross-bracing also prevented Denise from a clear shot at the assassin. Ignoring the pounding of her heart and the sweat of her slick palms, she edged closer.

Don't look down. One mistake could lead to a fall and death.

Her foot slipped. Her stomach plummeted to her knees. Her purse tilted and the gun flew out. And Denise fell toward the stage.

YVONNE GLANCED OVER her shoulder and squinted into the light. So the woman had followed her. Good.

Yvonne enjoyed a challenge, but the P.I.'s meddling had caused more difficulties than she liked. She should have shot them outside Martin's home while she was impersonating the cook. But her orders were specific. Ford was to die on the stage while he made his speech.

This time, Yvonne wouldn't fail. She'd collect payment in full. In the confusion after her shot, she'd take out the woman. She peered over her shoulder and grinned. An additional shot might not be necessary.

The P.I. was off balance. Falling.

Good.

DENISE SPREAD HER ARMS, twisted and grasped an I beam. Gripping the metal tight, she swung back onto the brace. Sheesh, that had been close. But she didn't have time to wait for her violently accelerated pulse to settle.

Without her weapon, she had to sneak up on Yvonne, hoping the assassin did not spy her first. She peered through the I beams and noted that Yvonne, facing the other direction, had stopped in a crouch, bracing herself at a steel intersection.

Time was running out. Denise risked larger steps

and prayed for balance, prayed she could stop her in time.

Yvonne removed her gun from a sling across her back. She lifted the weapon.

Sighted her target.

With less than a second to prevent Ford's death, Denise lunged. Her elbow knocked the gun from Yvonne's hands. The assassin cursed and teetered on the I beam.

Denise spun and tumbled. She flung out her arms, desperate to grasp a handhold. But her hands clutched only air.

With a thud, Denise's body slammed into a crossbar. The wind knocked out of her lungs. Dizzily clutching hold, she tried to pull herself up.

Like a cat, Yvonne regained her balance. She jumped onto the beam where Denise clung precariously. With an unruffled and detached expression, Yvonne raised her foot and stomped, aiming for Denise's vulnerable fingers. Denise moved her hand, narrowly avoiding a fall. She looked right, left, over her shoulder in search of a safe perch to swing to.

Only thirty feet of air lay between her and the hay bales below.

Yvonne stomped again.

At the excruciating pain in her fingers, Denise let go with one hand.

Denise knew she was going to die. Would Ford mourn her? Would he realize how much she loved him? At least the assassin couldn't shoot Ford without her weapon.

Appealing for mercy to the assassin's good side was useless. Yvonne didn't have a good side. She had not one sympathetic glimmer in her eyes. Pulling a revolver from a pocket, she raised her foot again.

At the sight of the gun, Denise knew she was about to die for nothing. She'd failed. The Black Rose would knock her to the floor, shoot and kill Ford, too. They would both die.

The assassin stomped once more, aiming for Denise's remaining hand that gripped the bar. Using all her strength, Denise swung her free hand into Yvonne's ankle, misdirecting the blow.

Unprepared for Denise's attack, Yvonne lost her balance. She gasped and fell, clutching at Denise who barely grasped the beam with her hurt hand. Clenching her teeth, Denise hung on, her arms aching from the additional weight of supporting them both.

Yvonne's grip slipped. And loosened. While Denise clung to the beam with her last strength, Yvonne soundlessly plunged to the stage below.

ON STAGE, FORD'S FEET vibrated. Something was very wrong. With a promise to return to the microphone soon, he interrupted his speech and asked Martin to explain the company's future plans to the stockholders.

Ford hurried backstage in search of Denise. The thump on the stage had sounded like someone had fallen. He glanced up and his heart leaped into his throat. A woman was dangling from an I beam. Although he didn't recognize her clothing, the sight of her golden hair had him trembling.

Before he shouted for her to hold on, she swung onto the beam. He didn't breathe as she slid down a pole attached to the wall to the stage.

Questions pummeled him. What had possessed her to go up there? How had she gotten there? Didn't she know if she'd fallen, she would have died?

He crossed the stage to join her and he tripped. Glancing down impatiently, he saw a gun. And beside the weapon, draped across a hay bale lay Yvonne's body.

The Black Rose had found a way around the guards and bullet-proof glass. Once again, somehow Denise had risked her life to save his. What an amazing woman!

"Are you all right?" he asked, taking her into his arms, running his hands over her to make sure she wasn't hurt.

She flung herself against him. "I was so afraid she'd shoot before I reached her." Her pulse jumped at the knowledge that Ford hadn't been injured. He looked wonderful. Relief and joy swept through her and a great happiness invaded her senses.

Ford tightened his embrace. She didn't want him ever to let go.

"When I saw you hanging up there, I thought I had lost you," he said in the tenderest of tones. "Are you sure you're all right?"

She nodded. "My hand is a little sore, but the Doctor and another of his men are hurt. And one's dead. We need to call an ambulance and the police."

"You scared the life out me, woman. What ever possessed you to go after her alone?"

"There was no time to find help. Once I realized she planned to shoot from behind the glass... How did she *know* about the glass?"

While she felt as if she'd been in battle for hours,

in reality only minutes had passed. Martin was still speaking to the stockholders. The audience knew nothing of the struggle behind the curtain since the sound of the Black Rose's fall had been deadened by the hay bales. Ford steered her past the broken body, and Denise looked away from the gruesome sight.

The Black Rose was finally dead.

"She didn't bother with a disguise," Denise said, wondering why she didn't feel happier. Rhonda's death had been avenged. Denise and Ford were now free to go on with their lives. She should be triumphant, but instead, sadness gripped her.

Ford picked up her fallen gun and handed it to her. When she didn't take it, he slipped it into his jacket pocket and turned to a bodyguard. "Call the police and an ambulance."

"Yes, sir." The guard walked away.

Perhaps she was just tired. But one question burned in Denise's mind. "How did Yvonne discover the bullet-proof glass?"

"Maybe she spied the glass truck and was suspicious," Ford suggested.

"I don't think so. She didn't wear a disguise and that meant she *planned* to use the ceiling passage to go behind the glass. She knew what we'd planned *before* she showed up today. The Doctor thinks she set a trap yesterday in the light switch that knocked out an agent. She'd carefully cased the scene before today."

Denise clung to Ford, hoping the Doctor's injured man would recover. In truth, she was numb. The worry over saving Ford's life, the fight to crawl through the black tunnel and then the near fall with

Yvonne tugging her had sapped the last of her strength. Shock and fatigue deadened her emotions.

One of the guards approached. "Both ambulance and police are on their way."

Ford put his arm around her shoulder. "Come on, we ought to get some ice on your hand."

"Don't go far," the guard said. "The police will question all of us. But don't worry. There's no need for the audience to know what's happened."

Ford nodded, then led her around the side of the stage. Up front, Martin still spoke. As she leaned into Ford's side, grateful for his strength and support, she realized he would soon leave her and retake his rightful place. "For how long can Martin take over the meeting?"

"About an hour."

She glanced at her watch. Only fifteen minutes had passed since Ford had started to speak—it seemed like years.

He must have felt her trembling. He spoke softly, taking complete control as if she were a child, and she didn't mind one bit. Grateful to have him to lean on, she rested her head on his arm. She didn't want to talk to the cops. She didn't want to think about the Black Rose. She didn't want to think about tomorrow.

Ford led her into a kitchen off the stage. He seated her by a table and opened a freezer. "No ice."

"I'll be fine." She wasn't. Not really. Her fingers had swelled and pain followed the swelling.

Ford reached into the freezer. "Someone left an ice pack in here." He wrapped it in a paper towel and handed the cold pack to her, his eyes haunted with an emotion she couldn't name. "Are any of your fingers broken?"

"The joints are fine. It's the swelling under the nails that hurts. I'll get over it. Aren't you going to answer the stockholders' questions?"

He looked straight into her eyes. "I'd rather stay with you." His heated glance loosened the knot in her stomach.

"I'm not going anywhere," she told him.

The guard stuck his head in the kitchen. "The cops have agreed to wait until after the meeting to question you."

"Thanks," Ford said.

The guard jerked his thumb in the direction of the stage. "There's a young man outside who says the holographic equipment is ready for a test run."

Ford nodded but didn't leave her. He hovered as if he thought she was as delicate as porcelain while she peeled off the makeup. "You brought the holographic equipment to the stockholders' meeting?"

He watched her closely. "I wasn't sure the equipment would arrive in time. A demonstration will be more convincing than any speech. But it can wait."

Strength returned to her limbs. "Did my little aerial act scare the sense out of you?"

"What?" His eyes widened in surprise.

"You wouldn't have flown that equipment in and arranged a demonstration if you didn't think it was important. The stockholders are here. You need the votes. Go."

"I'm not abandoning you."

"Fine." She rose to her feet. "I'll come along."

He reached out and placed his hands on her shoulders. "I'm not saying this right. That equipment isn't as important to me as you are."

Her heart lifted with hope. She wanted him to tell her how he felt about her. She planted a kiss in the crook of his neck. "You can love us both—me and your precious equipment. Just as long as I'm the one you hold in your arms at night."

Chapter Thirteen

The police questions and investigation had taken hours. While Ford had remained with Denise, they'd learned that the Doctor and the injured guard were expected to recover fully.

Ford had never returned to the stage for his demonstration or to finish his speech, either, but Martin had done a fine job of covering for him. A month ago, a "fine job" wouldn't have been good enough— but a month ago he'd hadn't known Denise, a month ago he hadn't loved her. No way would he leave her after what she'd been through to save his life. It had taken all her courage to crawl through that tunnel to save him. When she'd almost fallen, he'd vowed if she survived he would always put her first, before his many businesses.

He didn't bother asking himself how he had changed so incredibly in such a short time. The full effect of her on every aspect of his life was incalculable, wonderful and irrevocable. She hadn't only been the catalyst, she was the constant stimulus that kept him feeling alive. Long ago, he'd learned there were no guarantees, and though he wasn't sure she reciprocated his feelings, he hoped she shared his devouring need for them to be together.

Although the stockholders' meeting and the subsequent police investigation had run late into the evening, Ford had asked the board members to come to Norton Industries tonight for a special technical presentation. But first, he had a private demonstration for Denise. As he steered her to a windowless room at Norton Industries, empty except for a few folding chairs and assorted machinery, he flashed her a mischievous smile.

While a technician warmed up the holographic equipment taking up most of the available floor space, Ford watched Denise. Earlier, she had been pale and weary during the police investigation, but now, color had returned to her face, and her tawny eyes observed the equipment with lively interest. She leaned forward boldly, missing nothing, and he'd bet she could duplicate the technician's adjustments if necessary. She had a knack for asking marvelous questions until she solved whatever puzzle she was working on. He admired how her mind focused and he adored how she stirred him to life with her extraordinary sensuality.

She fascinated him and he could stare at her for hours.

When he'd seen her hanging above the stage, his heart had palpitated, his stomach churned. He never wanted to go through that kind of agony again.

By God, he'd known right then that he'd fallen in love with his wife's cousin. Odd how the two women were so different. Rhonda had taken pleasure in pleasing him, and he'd protected and sheltered her. Denise didn't need him to take care of her, and her strength was part of what attracted him. He loved Denise like an equal partner, both of them giving and taking.

While he could never forget Rhonda, he had finally let go of the past. Instead of the aching loneliness, energy pumped through his veins. As he sensed Rhonda would be thrilled, a lump lodged in his throat. He was a lucky man, fortunate to have two such women in his life, two completely different loves. Both priceless. Denise couldn't walk out of his life without him attempting to persuade her otherwise.

And he could be very persuasive.

Denise glanced at him and must have sensed his misty-eyed sentiments. She lifted a finger to trace the crease on his forehead. "I didn't know machinery could bring tears to your eyes."

"But you do know I always pursue what I want?"

She placed her hands on her hips and issued a throaty challenge. "I suspect the entire free world knows you go after what you want."

He chuckled. "Good. Then you know resistance is hopeless."

"Mmm." She licked her lip, indicating her nervousness. "We aren't talking about the machinery, are we?"

"Excuse me, sir," the tech interrupted. "The system is ready to go. You have time for a test."

The tech held out a microphone and pointed to the equipment. "When you want to shut her down, just press this button."

As the technician waved goodbye, Ford turned back to Denise. He pointed to a room down the hallway. "Let's go into the conference room and have a look before the board members arrive."

The conference room had huge windows with a skyline view of New Orleans and a marble table with leather chairs to seat thirty people, but her eyes were drawn to the four video cameras mounted on each wall of the room. Ford flicked on the remote and a red light on the cameras indicated they were now filming. He used another switch and she and Ford suddenly filled a large-screen television behind the table.

On-screen, Ford looked superbly handsome in a navy suit, white pin-striped shirt and maroon tie. "The camera records our every movement. Then the equipment in the other room plays it back but meanwhile, it's storing three-dimensional images to make the holograms."

When he approached and kneeled at her feet, her heart cartwheeled at his silliness. Now what was he up to?

"Give me your hand."

She did as he asked, glancing at the television screen at the far end of the table to catch their images.

"Marry me?" he asked, the timbre of his voice sugar-soft.

She laughed in delight. "Sure. You'll make the perfect husband. I'll always control the TV remote. And if I have any trouble with you, I'll turn you off."

His eyes gleamed with a look hot enough to melt steel. "I can't imagine ever being turned off by you."

Still smiling, she leaned forward to kiss him.

"Excuse me." Martin strode into the room, interrupting their banter. His suit and shirt were rumpled. His face was drenched with perspiration. "There you are, Ford. I really think the board is annoyed at having to return tonight, especially after you abandoned them.''

Ford rose to his feet. "You did a good job, filling in for me.''

Not the least bit mollified, Martin scowled petulantly. "But they wanted you. They always want you. Whatever you had to say should have been said at the next board meeting.''

"We need to move on this technology now. I want it in production soon.''

Martin stabbed his finger toward Ford. "It's always what you want. You'll bankrupt the company if you don't stop dreaming.''

"There's nothing wrong with dreams," Ford replied mildly.

Embarrassed that Martin had heard their silliness, Denise remained silent, observing the two men. Martin appeared agitated. When he spoke, he gestured wildly.

"There's plenty wrong with dreams," he said. "You'll overextend the company. We're ripe for a takeover. Yesterday, our unknown buyer bought another three percent of Norton.''

Ford stilled, his expression unreadable, but his blue eyes darkening. "Now, Martin. I've always counted on you to keep us on solid financial ground.''

"Don't you patronize me. You aren't the one who spends sleepless nights wondering where to find the capital to pay our bills. And that holographic equipment will never work.''

"It won't?" Ford laughed and folded his arms over his chest.

"This is no laughing matter. You've never considered me more than a bean counter."

"That's not true. I need your help. I couldn't run this company without your steadfast ideas."

"Bull!" Martin withdrew a gun from inside his jacket. "Yvonne was supposed to kill you."

"But Yvonne's dead. There's no need for weapons to defend ourselves." Ford spoke calmly. "Put that gun away."

Denise's mouth went dry at the suddenly threatening look in Martin's wild eyes, the malicious twist of his mouth. Martin wasn't carrying a gun for protection. He looked ready to shoot.

She and Ford were too far from the door to flee. Not close enough to attack before Martin pulled the trigger.

But Martin's attention was on Ford. If she edged toward the door and called for help, maybe Ford could stall him. And if Martin knew she'd gotten away, he might hesitate to shoot.

"Well, Yvonne may have failed. But *I* won't." Martin lifted the gun and aimed at Ford.

Ford didn't move. "*You* hired Yvonne? How does a by-the-book guy like you hook up with an assassin?"

Martin smiled. "Henschel was approached about selling the clinic's embryos on the black market. He said he'd consider it if the man put him in touch with an assassin for hire. Before he killed himself, Henschel passed Yvonne's phone number to me."

Denise inched toward the door. No wonder the Black Rose had found Grendal in Switzerland and followed them to Neuchâtel. Ford had phoned Martin

who had told Yvonne their whereabouts. Martin and
Dr. Henschel had hired Yvonne. They'd joined together against a common enemy. Dr. Henschel
needed Ford and Rhonda dead to protect his reputation when he'd mixed up the embryos. And with Ford
dead, Martin could take control of Norton Industries.
But he had to be careful about having Ford killed too
soon after Henschel's death because Martin hadn't
wanted the Black Rose tied to him. So he'd instructed
Yvonne to wait until he'd given her the go-ahead.

Yvonne hadn't given up on the contract because
she'd expected Martin to pay her. And Martin had
arranged to let the Black Rose into his home where
she'd left the roses on the pillows. Every time Ford
had called the office, Martin had told the Black Rose
their plans.

She'd almost reached the door when Martin spun
toward her, the gun aimed at her heart. "You're not
going anywhere."

Denise froze, wishing for the bullet-proof vest
she'd taken off after the Black Rose's death.

"She has nothing to do with this," Ford demanded.
"Let her go." Ford stepped closer to Martin. "Did
you hire Denise to kidnap me?"

Oh, God. White-hot fear flashed through her. She'd
expected Ford to divert Martin's attention but not by
putting himself at even greater risk. Not by accusing
her of betrayal.

Ford thought she was in on this, too. His accusation
hurt worse than her swollen and stomped-on fingers.
She raised her head and blinked back tears. Ford
wasn't looking at her. His eyes were cold, hard, fearless as he wrung information from his partner.

"The timing couldn't have been better," Martin crowed. "You'd cleared your schedule for a honeymoon, so I took advantage of the situation."

Knowing she might only have one chance to flee, Denise tensed and waited for the perfect moment.

Martin's hand shook. "I've never had the pleasure of killing anyone by my own hand."

"I thought we were friends," Ford said sadly.

Denise coiled her muscles as she realized Ford was drawing Martin's attention to him. If Martin pulled the trigger, she'd make her move. Readying herself, she breathed shallowly.

Martin's voice rose an octave. "I'll shoot you in the gut. I'll enjoy watching you die, hotshot."

"Why the hostility, Martin? You own as much stock as I do. You run the company most of the time." Ford's tone was soft and nonthreatening. If his intent was to distract Martin from her, his tactic was working.

"Exactly. I run the company and do all the grunt work while you take the credit." Martin's dispassionate voice contrasted with the fire blazing in his eyes. "You scheme to be in charge. In control. Dr. Henschel wanted your position on the board at the Kine clinic but you took that away from him. But you aren't stealing my dream from me. Tomorrow, I'll be president of Norton Industries."

At his threat, a chill shivered down her back. Any second now, Martin would shoot. His voice had reached a singsongy pitch. His face and neck flushed angry red. "You've insulted me for the last time."

Ford raised his hand, still holding the remote control.

Martin cocked the gun, pointed it at Ford and pulled the trigger. "Die!"

Ford hurled the remote at Martin's face and rolled. Denise ducked. Gunshots pierced the room, whining in succession, slamming into padded chairs, the desk, a video camera.

Denise lunged toward the door. Out of the corner of her eye she spied Ford duck under the table.

"Bastard!" Martin hurled the empty gun in frustration, yanked out a knife and dived after Denise.

Her last glance to assure herself of Ford's safety slowed her. With a painful jerk of her hair, Martin yanked her against his chest. He raised an evilly glinting knife to her throat as Ford lunged out from beneath the conference table.

"Take another step and she's dead."

Denise didn't hesitate. She raised her hands to grip either side of Martin's knife hand, braced her arms and ducked beneath the weapon. At the same time, she stomped on his toe with her heel.

Twisting to the side, she forced Martin to drop the knife. He plunged to the floor, scrambling on hands and knees. She shifted to kick the weapon away.

"Watch out!" Ford yelled a warning at the trash can Martin tossed in her path.

She couldn't stop her momentum that fast. As she and the receptacle collided, she tumbled.

Martin grabbed the knife and jumped to his feet, thrusting the blade straight at Ford. Her heart slammed into her ribs and from her back, she stuck out her foot, tripping Martin. Ford rammed his fist into Martin's jaw so hard the man's neck snapped back and he collapsed, his eyes rolling back in his head.

"Are you okay?" Ford asked, holding out a hand to help her up.

She nodded, ignored his hand, pulled herself to her feet and walked away. It was over.

Whatever she'd hoped was between them had just died, leaving her in despair. If he believed Martin had hired her and that she had any part in this murder plot, he wasn't the man she thought. Or the man she wanted.

He'd shattered her last illusion. Her desperate last hope he might love her was now no more than an adolescent romanticism she should have been left behind long ago. With his accusation the past was now irrevocably behind her.

"Where are you going?" he asked, a guarded look in his eyes.

"Away." Away from him. Her throat tightened with tears but she wouldn't give in to them. She had her pride and drew it around her like a shield. But pride would be little consolation during the long lonely years that stretched ahead of her without Ford.

A hand clamped over her shoulder. "You aren't leaving me this easy."

"Let go." Her tone was uncharacteristically harsh, so she wasn't surprised when he removed his hand.

But she was totally unprepared when he shifted in front of her, blocking her path on his powerful legs, his black hair, as usual, neat but with a stray loose lock on his forehead balancing the sharpness of his chiseled cheekbones, his penetrating eyes assessing her with a you-cannot-hide-from-me look. "I never thought you knew the details of Martin's scheme."

The harrowing tension of the last few minutes, and his shameful accusation that she'd conspired with Martin, led to a gloomy despondency she barely restrained. She strangled back a moan and tried to step around him, but he shifted and again obstructed her departure.

He crossed his arms over his chest and stared down at her, his temper with her clearly mounting. "Martin hired many people to do his dirty work. Not every one of them intended to murder me. No doubt, only a few knew his plans. The Doctor and his men obviously weren't in on his schemes. He used them. And he used you."

At the realization Martin *might* have hired her, she staggered. Ford brought her to his chest and whispered into her hair. "It doesn't matter. If he hired you, then at least he did one good thing for me. He brought you into my life. And I intend to make it permanent."

Excitement, then doubt, filled her. Ford was just full of surprises. But did he mean it? "I thought you could never replace Rhonda?"

"I can't. She will always have a special place in my heart. You aren't a replacement. You are the woman I love now. I want us to be together for the rest of our lives. And I think Rhonda would be happy for us."

"Say that again, please."

"Rhonda would—"

"Not that part." Unamused, she tapped her foot impatiently, trying not to go mushy inside as her heart swelled with love for this dear and magnificent man.

His blue eyes twinkled. "You want to hear the part about being together—"

"Guess again."

He chuckled and leaned forward to kiss her. "I love you. I want to marry you." His tone purred deliciously in her ear, and while his expression was serious, she was surprised and gladdened to hear a taut tremor in his voice.

"Marry?" She flung her arms around his neck and drew him close, her heart soaring with joy.

He tightened his arms, enfolding her protectively. "Of course, marry. I want to spend the rest of my life with you."

Hope and happiness gushed inside her with a force so strong, she caught her breath in wonder. "And as usual, you intend to have your way?"

"Damned right."

"Cute attitude, Ford. Real cute."

One brow lifted as he flashed her a sinfully delicious wink while his hands drifted to her bottom and cradled her against his hips. "I'm looking forward to having my way with you."

"You'll only hear one objection from me."

"Really?"

"What's taking so long?"

Epilogue

Ford had warned her the Braddack family gathering was nothing to worry about, but she'd still been nervous about meeting his parents as his fiancée. What would they think of a woman who'd kidnapped their son from his wedding? Would they object to Ford's making her his head of security at Norton Industries?

She'd dressed with care, hoping to make a good impression. But worry gnawed her.

She hated parties and the sounds of the jazz band on the front lawn did nothing to calm her frazzled nerves. The minute Ford drove up to his parents' summer home, Denise knew why he'd laughed at her when she'd asked if her casual skirt and blouse were suitable. Swirling colors drew her attention from the two-story farmhouse to crowds of people attired in everything from ratty jeans to Armani suits, and all of them seemingly jubilant. Dogs chased a Frisbee. A boy flew a kite, while other kids with glazed eyes played some kind of virtual reality game on the front porch. The delicious scent of crawfish gumbo and barbecue made her salivate, and for the first time that morning her mouth wasn't dry.

At the thought of meeting the Braddack clan, her stomach churned. Ford parked the car and steered her to a barbecue pit where a tall, broad-shouldered man with salt-and-pepper hair, his tanned chest glistening with the effort of turning a spitted pig, removed his work gloves and handed his job to an assistant. He wiped himself down with a towel, threw on a golf shirt, then picked up a cocktail and embraced Ford. Even if they'd never met at Rhonda's wedding and funeral, Denise would have recognized his father, Red.

A moment later, Red caught her by surprise with the same bear hug and back patting he'd used on his son. "Welcome to the family."

Eva, a delicate-looking woman wearing a long skirt, a flowered silk blouse with a diamond daisy pinned to the collar, took Red's arm and gently separated him from Denise. "I don't think Ford will appreciate it if you suffocate the poor girl," Ford's mother said.

Grateful for Eva's interference, Denise grinned her thanks.

Ford's face creased in a happy smile. "Mom, come say hello to Denise."

Ford had told Denise so much about his mother that she felt as though she knew Eva well. While she thought she'd been prepared for almost any reaction—from warm approval to cold disdain—she'd never imagined the reality.

Eva leaned against her husband's side, her intelligent eyes revealing strain, her knuckles white as she clenched her fists. "I'm going to get this over with and confess."

"Confess?" Ford asked.

"And I hope you'll both forgive me," his mother continued.

Red kissed the top of his wife's head. "You didn't?"

"I did." Eva's eyes kept their tense look.

Ford's forehead wrinkled. "Mother?"

In tense confusion, Denise looked from Ford's frown to his mother's anxiety-laden face to Red's twinkling gaze. "Are you all talking in some family code I have to decipher?"

Eva reached out and with surprising strength took her hand and one of Ford's. "I hired you to kidnap my son."

Flabbergasted, Denise's mouth dropped open. The belief that she'd been working for Martin Crewsdale had nipped her with guilt. No matter how often Ford told her it didn't matter, she couldn't shake the feeling that she'd unknowingly betrayed him.

Since Denise had never known her client's identity, she'd feared Martin had hired her to do his dirty work. To find out otherwise was a giant relief. Martin had had nothing to do with her assignment to kidnap Ford. She'd been working for Eva Braddack, Ford's mother!

A worried look darkened Eva's eyes. "I hid my identity by hiring you by mail and paying you with cash."

"How did you arrange for my plane and pilot?" Ford asked in a neutral tone.

"I simply told the pilot you'd asked me to have him ready to leave."

Beside her, Ford's entire body shook with mirth.

"Mom, let me guess. You couldn't let me make the mistake of marrying Lindsay?"

"She wasn't right for you."

"I'll drink to that." Red hooted with laughter and thrust a beer into Denise's hand. "Drink up."

She brought the beer to her mouth and then stopped herself. In her astonishment, she'd forgotten she shouldn't drink alcohol for a while. Denise had worried herself almost sick. She'd thought Eva would never forgive her for putting her son in danger. But it had been Eva's idea to kidnap Ford in the first place.

Ford's famous mother seemed to be waiting for Denise's forgiveness. "It's okay," she murmured to reassure Eva, a weight lifting from her shoulders. "You hired me to kidnap Ford out of love."

At her words, Eva squeezed her hand. The strain left her eyes. She smiled at Denise warmly.

The Louisiana heat, combined with Eva's confession, suddenly seemed too much to assimilate. Dizzy, Denise dropped the bottle from numb fingers, her knees buckled. Ford scooped her into his arms.

"I'm sorry, I shocked you," Eva muttered. "Ford, take her into the shade." She snagged a giggling curly-haired child from a group of roaming kids. "Skye, please go get your new aunt a glass of cool water."

Seeing the commotion, Ford's identical twin, Max, strode over with his wife, Brooke, who was very obviously pregnant. Brooke nodded hello, her lips turning into a wide grin at Ford's possessive grip on Denise. "Welcome to the family."

"Ditto," Max said. "I, too, have a confession to make."

"Yes?" Ford's eyebrow arched. Max's eyebrow went up in an identical movement.

"You're looking at your newest stockholder," Max admitted with a sheepish grin. "I figured I couldn't put my money into a better company."

Max had been buying up Norton Industries stock. Ford broke into a wider grin, and Denise knew he couldn't ask for a more inventive partner than his brilliant brother. But Denise didn't say a word, feeling silly in an attempt to carry on a conversation from her position in Ford's arms.

"Hope you forgive me for horning in on Ford's success," Max said to Denise.

"Why should I mind? He'll probably put you to work. But I'll consider us even if you can convince him I'm perfectly capable of walking."

Brooke chuckled. "The men in this family adore any excuse to sweep women off their feet."

"Ford, please put me down. I've never fainted in my life, and I'm not going to start just because I'm pregnant."

Oops.

She'd meant to tell him in private, not in the middle of a family gathering, but the words had just slipped out. She realized with Ford's loving support, social gatherings no longer intimidated her, and she felt happy and at ease.

At the news, Max clapped Ford on the back. Brooke sent her an approving smile. Red danced Eva off in an exaggerated jitterbug.

To his credit, Ford didn't drop her. He didn't put

her down, either. "The doctor told me I couldn't have children," he said.

Denise arched her eyebrow. "The doctor lied. I suspect it was just one more way for the Kine clinic to get back at you. Only this deception turned out rather sweet."

"I'm going to be a father?" His voice trembled in wonder, his eyes soft and dreamy.

She snuggled against his chest. "A father and a husband, although I'd prefer the order was reversed."

"Don't worry, sweetheart, once my mother goes into action, she'll have us married quickly."

Her eyes rounded. "How quickly?"

"The sooner the better, but she'll probably insist on a gigantic society wedding."

She peered at him hopefully. "We could always elope."

"And spoil my mother's fun?" His arms tightened around her, and he laughed all the way into a kiss. "This is one wedding I don't want to be kidnapped from."

EVER HAD ONE OF THOSE DAYS?

TO DO:

☑️ late for a super-important meeting, you discover the cat has eaten your panty hose

☑️ while you work through lunch, the rest of the gang goes out and finds a one-hour, once-in-a-lifetime 90% off sale at the most exclusive store in town (Oh, and they also get to meet Brad Pitt who's filming a movie across the street.)

☑️ you discover that your intimate phone call with your boyfriend was on company-wide intercom

☑️ finally at the end of a long and exasperating day, you escape from it all with an entertaining, humorous and always romantic Love & Laughter book!

ENJOY

EVERY DAY!

For a preview, turn the page....

The plan would come together. The black Rose

Here's a sneak peek at
Colleen Collins's RIGHT CHEST, WRONG NAME
Available August 1997...

———————

"DARLING, YOU SOUND like a broken cappuccino machine," murmured Charlotte, her voice oozing disapproval.

Russell juggled the receiver while attempting to sit up in bed, but couldn't. If he *sounded* like a wreck over the phone, he could only imagine what he looked like.

"What mischief did you and your friends get into at your bachelor's party last night?" she continued.

She always had a way of saying "your friends" as though they were a pack of degenerate water buffalo. Professors deserved to be several notches higher up on the food chain, he thought. Which he would have said if his tongue wasn't swollen to twice its size.

"You didn't do anything...bad...did you, Russell?"

"Bad." His laugh came out like a bark.

"Bad as in *naughty.*"

He heard her piqued tone but knew she'd never admit to such a base emotion as jealousy. Charlotte Maday, the woman he was to wed in a week, came from a family who bled blue. Exhibiting raw emotion was akin to burping in public.

After agreeing to be at her parents' pool party by noon, he untangled himself from the bed sheets and stumbled to the bathroom.

"Pool party," he reminded himself. He'd put on his best front and accommodate Char's request. Make the family rounds, exchange a few pleasantries, play the role she liked best: the erudite, cultured English literature professor. After fulfilling his duties, he'd slink into some lawn chair, preferably one in the shade, and nurse his hangover.

He tossed back a few aspirin and splashed cold water on his face. Grappling for a towel, he squinted into the mirror.

Then he jerked upright and stared at his reflection, blinking back drops of water. "Good Lord. They stuck me in a wind tunnel."

His hair, usually neatly parted and combed, sprang from his head as though he'd been struck by lightning. "Can too many Wild Turkeys do that?" he asked himself as he stared with horror at his reflection.

Something caught his eye in the mirror. Russell's gaze dropped.

"What in the—"

Over his pectoral muscle was a small patch of white. A bandage. Gingerly, he pulled it off.

Underneath, on his skin, was not a wound but a small, neat drawing.

"A red heart?" His voice cracked on the word *heart*. Something—a word?—was scrawled across it.

"Good Lord," he croaked. "I got a tattoo. A heart tattoo with the name Liz on it."

Not Charlotte. Liz!

HARLEQUIN WOMEN KNOW ROMANCE WHEN THEY SEE IT.

And they'll see it on **ROMANCE CLASSICS**, the new 24-hour TV channel devoted to romantic movies and original programs like the special **Harlequin® Showcase of Authors & Stories**.

The **Harlequin® Showcase of Authors & Stories** introduces you to many of your favorite romance authors in a program developed exclusively for Harlequin® readers.

Watch for the **Harlequin® Showcase of Authors & Stories** series beginning in the summer of 1997.

ROMANCE CLASSICS

If you're not receiving ROMANCE CLASSICS, call your local cable operator or satellite provider and ask for it today!

Escape to the network of your dreams.

Take 4 bestselling love stories FREE

Plus get a FREE surprise gift!

Special Limited-time Offer

Mail to Harlequin Reader Service®

3010 Walden Avenue
P.O. Box 1867
Buffalo, N.Y. 14240-1867

YES! Please send me 4 free Harlequin Intrigue® novels and my free surprise gift. Then send me 4 brand-new novels every month. Bill me at the low price of $2.94 each plus 25¢ delivery and applicable sales tax, if any.* That's the complete price and a savings of over 10% off the cover prices—quite a bargain! I understand that accepting the books and gift places me under no obligation ever to buy any books. I can always return a shipment and cancel at any time. Even if I never buy another book from Harlequin, the 4 free books and the surprise gift are mine to keep forever.

181 BPA A3UQ

Name	(PLEASE PRINT)	
Address	Apt. No.	
City	State	Zip

This offer is limited to one order per household and not valid to present Harlequin Intrigue® subscribers. *Terms and prices are subject to change without notice. Sales tax applicable in N.Y.

UINT-696

©1990 Harlequin Enterprises Limited

HARLEQUIN®

I N T R I G U E®

Everyone's talking about

THE ROSE TATTOO

Next month,
visit The Rose Tatoo and meet

THE WRONG MAN
by Kelsey Roberts

Her best friend is missing and Haley Jenkins is
determined to find her...without help from the police
department, and especially not from Dalton Ross,
the dynamic officer assigned to the case.
Haley knows he's the wrong man for the job...
but is he the right man for her?

**Be sure not to miss
THE WRONG MAN—it's Kelsey Roberts's
sixth and most spine-tingling Rose Tattoo yet!**

HE SAID

♥

SHE SAID

Explore the mystery of male/female communication in
this extraordinary new book from two of your favorite
Harlequin authors.

Jasmine Cresswell and Margaret St. George bring you the
exciting story of two romantic adversaries—each from
their own point of view!

DEV'S STORY. CATHY'S STORY.
As he sees it. As she sees it.
Both sides of the story!

The heat is definitely on, and these two can't stay out of
the kitchen!

Don't miss HE SAID, SHE SAID.
Available in July wherever Harlequin books are sold.

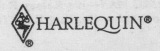

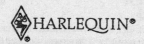

As Seen on TV!

Free Gift Offer

With a Free Gift proof-of-purchase
from any Harlequin® book, you can receive
a beautiful cubic zirconia pendant.

This stunning marquise-shaped stone is a genuine cubic
zirconia—accented by an 18" gold tone necklace.
(Approximate retail value $19.95)

Send for yours today...
compliments of ◈HARLEQUIN®

To receive your free gift, a cubic zirconia pendant, send us one original proof-of-purchase, photocopies not accepted, from the back of any Harlequin Romance®, Harlequin Presents®, Harlequin Temptation®, Harlequin Superromance®, Harlequin Intrigue®, Harlequin American Romance®, or Harlequin Historicals® title available at your favorite retail outlet, together with the Free Gift Certificate, plus a check or money order for $1.65 U.S./$2.15 CAN. (do not send cash) to cover postage and handling, payable to Harlequin Free Gift Offer. We will send you the specified gift. Allow 6 to 8 weeks for delivery. Offer good until December 31, 1997, or while quantities last. Offer valid in the U.S. and Canada only.

Free Gift Certificate

Name: _____

Address: _____

City: _____ State/Province: _____ Zip/Postal Code: _____

Mail this certificate, one proof-of-purchase and a check or money order for postage and handling to: HARLEQUIN FREE GIFT OFFER 1997. In the U.S.: 3010 Walden Avenue, P.O. Box 9071, Buffalo NY 14269-9057. In Canada: P.O. Box 604, Fort Erie, Ontario L2Z 5X3.